twinkle

A Chanukah Romance

Light My Candle
Book Two

allie lasky

one

. . .

Estee

THERE'S a used condom in my bathroom trash can.

My heart pounds as I take in the evidence as clinically as possible:

I've been away for the weekend, enjoying my friend Arielle's bachelorette party.

My fiancé and I haven't used condoms in two years.

Aaron has been distant the last few weeks, keeping his texts brief and distracted by his phone when he's home.

My stomach kicks, and absentmindedly I rub my hand over the swell of my belly. The little gremlin reacts immediately, more motion hammering at me insistently.

I think I'm going to be sick.

My head spins and my vision starts to go fuzzy. I lean against the bathroom counter and slowly urge myself down into a sitting position. My belly gets in the way and I have to shift a few times to get comfortable. It's like my heart is in my throat, acid spreading down my esophagus and into my chest like poison seeping into a river.

Reaching for my phone, I unlock it on muscle memory and speak into the voice command: "Call Asher."

My best friend answers on the third ring. "What's going on?"

"I need you." The words are punched out by a sob.

"Estee." His voice goes up in pitch. "Are you okay? Is it the baby?"

Taking a gulp of air, I try to stand up, but the world tilts sharply to the left. Slumping back onto the bathroom floor, I try to take shallow breaths.

"I need you to come pick me up."

"Did something happen?" He sounds worried. Fuck. I don't want him to worry about me. He has enough going on.

I close my eyes to recenter myself.

"Aaron slept with someone else." Saying the words sends a stab of pain through my chest. "I can't stay here."

There's a clatter on the other end. Asher murmurs something—I'm guessing to Arielle. They're never apart for very long.

"It's a four hour drive. Can you pack a bag?"

I nod, and then realizing he can't see me, repeat out loud. "Yeah."

"I love you, Estee," he says. "This isn't the end of the world. We'll get through this."

My hand falls to my swollen belly, smoothing over the bump.

"Promise?" My voice sounds weak and needy even to my own ears.

"I promise."

In what feels like no time, Asher and Arielle are bursting through the front door of my third floor walkup in Queens. They've brought a U-Haul with them all the way from Boston.

Asher is like a brother to me. Our mothers went through a Mommy & Me class together twenty-eight years ago and have been best friends ever since. Ash and I were born thirteen days apart. We've done everything together. He proposed to Arielle the weekend before Aaron proposed to me, and we've been coordinating the wedding planning to celebrate together rather than one of us outshining the other.

Arielle has been my best friend since we were six. She was the quiet, nerdy new girl to our school and I took an immediate shine to her. She's been there for me through thick and thin, through college and law school, and even though we live in two separate cities, we've only grown closer since she and Ash started dating two years ago.

She wraps me in a hug. I know she doesn't like hugs, so the fact that she's reaching out to me in this way is huge.

"I'm so sorry, Es," she says quietly.

"Me, too," I admit.

The front door opens and my fiancé waltzes through, texting.

He stops short at the sight of Asher holding a suitcase in each hand.

"What's going on?" Aaron asks.

Tilting my head, I study him. "Where've you been?"

"I was at the office," he says.

"On a Sunday night?" Arielle asks.

He shrugs, totally nonchalant. "I have a big case."

He's never been the biggest fan of Arielle. I'm not sure why. Her autism makes her direct and I don't think he likes that. He's definitely not fond of Asher.

Why did I want to pledge my life to a man who doesn't get along with my two best friends?

"Oh, I'm sure," I mutter, handing Arielle a tote bag. "Can you take this down to the truck?"

She nods, urging Asher to follow her. They leave us alone.

Aaron slams the front door shut.

"What the fuck is this?" he demands.

"I'm leaving."

"What? Why?"

"I don't know," I say blandly. "Maybe it has something to do with the used condom you left in the trash can."

His face goes white and then purple. "What are you talking about, you stupid bitch?"

My heart hammers rapidly like gunfire. "I've told you not to speak to me that way."

"I'll speak however I goddamn please," he snaps. "It's my fucking apartment."

"This conversation has ceased to be productive. I'm done."

Turning away, I reach for one of the bags.

Aaron catches my arm, his fingers digging in tightly.

"Don't you walk away from me."

My vision goes fuzzy again. I've never seen him like this. He has never put a hand on me—not once. In our five and a half years together, I never imagined myself in this type of situation.

The front door bangs open.

"Hey! Let her go!" Asher shouts.

Aaron scoffs. "Of course you called him."

But he does let me go. I rush to the other side of the room and Ash and Arielle wrap their arms around me.

"What's that supposed to mean?" I ask, protected by their presence.

"He's your knight in shining armor. He's the one that fixes everything." He sneers at me.

I snap. "Well, if you hadn't broken our relationship, there wouldn't be anything to fix."

"I didn't break shit." He rolls his eyes. "Always so dramatic."

Asher squeezes my arm. "It's not worth it. *He's* not worth this."

Swallowing, I point to the last two bags. "That's it. That's all that's left."

"You got it." Ash grabs the suitcases, hefting them toward

the door. He glances at Arielle, as if to warn her to stay with me.

Picking up my purse and the last tote bag, I'm almost at the door when Aaron calls after me.

"I want the ring back."

My eyebrows go up. "Excuse me?"

"You heard me, you freeloading bitch. I bought the ring."

"Yeah, and it's my grandmother's diamond. I know she gave it to you."

Yes, he did update the setting, putting the stone in a modern band.

"It's my ring," he demands.

My great-grandmother brought the original ring with her when she immigrated from Germany after World War I. It's a family heirloom.

But of course he wouldn't ever see it that way.

"Sue me for it," I tell him lightly.

two

. . .

Benji

WHEN ASHER CALLED me up and asked if I still had the spare room empty, this is *not* what I expected.

Esther Cohen is standing on my doorstep.

Estee.

She has nowhere to go.

"Hey, I'm Benji," I tell her, offering my hand.

"Applebaum." She clears her throat. "I remember."

I was a dick to her as a kid.

When I was a kid, they reinforced the idea that pulling pigtails means a boy likes a girl. It normalized abusive relationships. They teach kids now that when a boy is a jerk to a girl, it doesn't mean he likes her, it means he's being a jerk.

In my case, I did like her. I'd never seen a healthy adult relationship modeled for me, so I didn't know how to cope with my feelings other than by teasing her.

Growing up—and a shit ton of therapy—has made me see the error of my ways.

"Come on in," I tell her, holding the door open.

When she takes off her coat, my eyes are drawn to her rounded belly.

She's *pregnant*? My heart skips a beat. What is she doing here?

And then I catch sight of the bruises on her wrist.

My chest roars like a lion as acid tears through me. "Who did that to you?" I demand.

She flinches. "Nobody."

"Estee." I wait for her to meet my eyes. "Who is he?"

"He's not important. If I have my way, I'll never see him again," she says firmly.

I swallow. "You can stay as long as you'd like. As long as you need."

"I just need to get back on my feet," Estee says. "A few weeks, maybe."

"How far along are you?"

"Six months." She rubs her belly, almost as if she doesn't realize she's doing it.

"So you'll stay here, then," I decide.

She tilts her head. "What do you mean?"

"You're not moving with a newborn. That's ridiculous."

Her eyes flash. "I've just left one controlling asshole. I don't need another in my life."

Shit. I clear my throat.

"I just mean, you don't have to leave on my account. You can stay for as long as you need. Even after the baby's born."

She shudders. "I can't think about that."

"Look. The apartment is rent controlled. The spare bedroom is available. Don't rush to make any decisions," I tell her gently.

"I just landed on your doorstep. You can't seriously want a roommate *and* a baby–"

"I do," I tell her quietly.

She stares at me.

I don't want just any roommate. I want *her*.

I always have, ever since I was old enough to *like* a girl. Those six weeks at camp every summer were the best because

I got to see her every day. Growing up in Philadelphia and her in Chicago, we didn't have a lot of opportunities to see each other. My yearly trip to visit Asher for spring break sometimes afforded me a glimpse of her, but we didn't spend much time together.

It's not like I've been *pining* for her for the last fifteen years. She was my first crush. I grew up. So did she. I dated. I assume she did, too.

But all those feelings came rushing back the second I saw her again.

Her chestnut brown hair falls in gentle waves almost to her elbows. The front is pulled back into a clip, showing a layer of purple hair beneath it. Her makeup is light and natural, but her eyes are red, like she's been crying nonstop since Asher brought her back from New York two days ago.

"I'll be out of your hair soon enough," she says with a sigh. Her eyes flick up to mine, a rich amber rimmed by red. "Thanks for letting me stay."

"Anytime."

I really do mean it. I'd do pretty much anything she asked. It's sick, the pull she has over me after all these years.

Ushering her inside the apartment, I show her the spare room. Until recently, it was Asher's. Then he and Arielle decided to move in together. It makes sense; they're getting married in a few months.

But it left me all alone.

I don't want a stranger living with me. I've done that before; it's not great for my mental health. I don't want to have another meltdown.

Until I was diagnosed with OCD when I was fourteen, I didn't know there was a way to deal with the compulsions in a healthy way. All I knew was the overwhelming sense of helplessness. I didn't think I would ever get better. I didn't think I would ever be able to control it.

Therapy, medication, and a lot of work have brought me here. I like where I'm at now.

Will having a newborn in the house threaten all the work I've done?

Maybe.

But for Estee Cohen? Yeah, I'll do it anyway.

———

The office is my refuge these days.

Since Estee moved into my apartment two weeks ago, I've pulled a lot of extra overtime at the office, left early for nonexistent meetings, been late getting home. I'm trying to give her space. I'm trying to give *myself* space.

Her sweet perfume lingers in the house, filling the air with the scent of gardenias. I never thought I knew what gardenias smelled like. I do now.

There's a throw blanket thrown over the back of the couch. Her yogurt in the fridge and ten types of granola in the cupboard. She doesn't seem to keep any other food in the pantry.

I hope she's eating.

Ash gave me a very, *very* brief rundown of the situation. Her ex-fiancé got physical, she left, and she hasn't talked to him since. She hasn't said a word about it. Fuck, she's barely said three sentences to me that aren't directly about the living arrangements.

Every morning, I knock on her door, but when she tells me she's fine, I have to believe her. I don't know what else there is to do. She's a grown adult. Just because *I* want to take care of her doesn't mean she needs to be smothered.

When I make it to my desk, there's a bagel and a coffee already there. I peek over the cubicle walls. My neighbors aren't there.

Hmm.

Pushing the bagel to the edge of my desk, I evaluate the coffee. It's in a to-go container from the little café down the block. The handwriting scrawled on it does have my favorite order.

Worst case scenario, it's poison.

Best case scenario, it's my favorite coffee order.

I take a sip.

How long does it take for poison to kick in?

Busying myself with work, I dive into the research materials and prepare my case study. As a marketing psychologist, I get to spend most of my time deep in research and analysis, and only a little bit of time interacting with people.

People are weird.

I don't think I like people very much.

"Hey, B," Riv calls out around lunchtime.

I turn in my chair, my eyebrows already raised. "Yeah?"

"You coming out with us tonight?"

I purse my lips, deciding. I do like going to trivia at the pub a few blocks away. It's a fun, social way to unwind on my own terms. We keep the group pretty small.

Tonight, though…

My text chain with Asher pops up with a new message. He's worried about her.

I am, too.

He asks if we can meet up. It's not what I had planned for the night…

"No big if you want to stay in," Chet adds.

Rivka and Chet are my favorite coworkers, but even they don't know about my roommate. I have a feeling they wouldn't approve of my reasons for suddenly pulling overtime nights and weekends.

"Not tonight," I finally decide. "Maybe next time."

Replying to Asher's message, I let him know what time I'll be home.

"You okay, B?" Riv asks. Her face creases with concern. "You don't seem like yourself lately."

"I'll be fine," I tell her.

She frowns.

"I'm going through something."

"You want to talk about it?" she asks.

"Yeah, we're here for you," Chet chimes in.

Taking a deep breath, I hold it for three beats and then exhale.

"What do you do when your first love comes back into your life after fifteen years?"

He blinks at me.

"Oh, and she's pregnant, but her ex is an abusive asshole, so now she's crashing in your spare room?"

Riv shakes her head. "Don't fall in love with her."

"Why not?" Chet asks. "It's his first love. That would be, like—" He mimes a chef's kiss.

"She's got enough going on right now," I tell him. "The last thing she needs is me trying to swoop in and get her to fall for me."

"Why not? Don't you want her to?" he says.

Inhaling sharply, I count to three again before releasing.

"We're very different people than we were when I knew her. I was—unkind." I make a face. "I was an idiot. I need to make it up to her."

"You will," Chet says. "You've got this, bro."

Conversation finished, he goes back to his work, but Riv comes closer. She squeezes my shoulder.

"Don't fall in love with her," she warns again.

Shaking my head, I offer her a rueful grin. "Too late."

three

. . .

Estee

IN THREE SHORT WEEKS, I've figured out a system.

Benji leaves for work at 7:50 each morning. At 7:45, he knocks on my door and asks if I need anything.

I always tell him no.

Once he leaves, I set up at the kitchen table with my laptop, make a quick yogurt and granola, and dive into work.

In the evenings, I try to make myself scarce. I don't want to encroach on his space. He didn't ask for a roommate—I was basically foisted upon him.

Normally, I go for a walk to the shawarma place three blocks away with my laptop, fiddling around and making lists. After the dinner rush, I walk home and go straight to my room.

I'm not avoiding him. I just don't want to bother him.

Also, every time I see him, I think, *wow, Benji Applebaum has certainly glowed up.*

He went from a chubby, loud-mouthed kid with braces and acne to a genuine stud. He's about 5'8", thick around the middle with a solid layer of fluff, and his face is clear. And whew, what a face.

He's clean-shaven every day when he goes to work, but when he comes home in the evenings, I see the dusting of five o'clock shadow and it makes me wonder what he'd look like with a nice layer of scruff or maybe a full beard.

So it's not entirely for his own benefit that I'm avoiding him. He doesn't need a horny pregnant woman lusting after him in his own apartment. It seems like everything these days sets me off. Nobody told me being pregnant would make me want sex, like, all the time. I'm giving my toy collection an intense workout.

But today if I go outside, I think I might freeze to death and die. Or fall and hurt the baby and die.

It's the dreary part of November. Everyone is looking forward to Thanksgiving later this week. Except for me, that is.

My parents know that Aaron and I split, and they know I'm living with a friend of Asher's, but they don't know the reason why. They keep urging me to call him and work things out.

There is no *working things out* with an abuser. He didn't want the baby to begin with. I refuse to be tied to him for eighteen years.

I haven't decided whether I'll list his name on the birth certificate. Biologically, he's the father. Legally… well, if I put his name, he'll be able to sue for custody. Yes, I can get child support to help raise the baby, money that the baby is legally entitled to.

But it ties us together for eighteen years in the eyes of the law *and* it gives him another avenue to control me. He wasn't interested in anything to do with the baby's development or my health over the last six months.

He doesn't know where I am. My job is 100 percent remote, so I can work anywhere in the world. He could probably find out Asher's address and try to finagle it from him. My best friend has my back, though.

He always has.

When Benji walks into the apartment after work, he's followed by Asher, and my glum mood turns bright again.

"What are you doing here?" I ask. When I struggle to get up off the couch, he laughs and pulls me upright, then into his arms. "I thought you were going home."

As a teacher, he gets the entire week of Thanksgiving off work. Last I heard, he and Arielle were going to Chicago to be tourists in our home city before dealing with the families.

"Change in plans," Ash says, hugging me tightly. "Yoni and Elliott are hosting on Thursday. You're coming."

"I am?" I tease.

Asher nods. "Both of you."

Benji stops in the doorway, stricken. "What? No. I–"

"Sadie's family situation is… not good. We're doing a Friendsgiving this year instead," he says delicately.

Yoni is Asher's best friend and Elliott is Yoni's spouse—and Asher's ex. They're all very close still, which kind of weirds me out, but hey, it works for them. Yoni's brother is with Sadie, Arielle's friend and former roommate.

My hand falls to my bump. "Are you sure she wants me there? I barely know her."

"Yes. And *I* want you there," he says firmly. "Both of you."

My eyes meet Benji's. They're a rich hazel, bright and clear now that he's not wearing the Coke bottle-thick glasses he had growing up. I don't know if he got LASIK or if he's wearing contacts.

Asher clears his throat. "How are you feeling?"

"I'm fine," I tell him automatically.

"Are you eating enough?" Benji demands, his arms crossed over his broad chest.

"I'm *fine*," I say with more force.

"Your appetite is still off?" Asher asks gently.

Swallowing, I nod.

"Should I ask Elliott to make something special?"

"Don't put them out."

"That's not what I asked." Asher rubs my arm. "Do you need anything special?"

"I'm just going to throw it up two hours later anyways." I roll my eyes. "Yogurt is the only thing that stays down consistently. Sometimes applesauce."

Benji frowns. "That doesn't sound good."

"I'm nauseous, like, all the fucking time." I shrug a shoulder. "Not much I can do about it."

"They can't give you meds?"

This time, I laugh out loud. "I'm already taking the max dose. Hyperemesis gravidarum can last the entirety of a pregnancy. At this point, I just need to ride it out."

He hums, lost in thought.

"You'll be there," Asher inserts. "I don't care if you sit there and eat fucking applesauce, I don't want you to hide away all weekend."

"Yes, Daddy," I tease.

He gives a whole body shiver. "That is not cool, Es."

"I didn't think you had a Daddy kink, Ash," I taunt back.

"I don't. You know I don't like that." He shudders.

"Hey, no kink-shaming." I grin at my oldest friend. It always sets him off when people—especially adult women—call their fathers "Daddy." So of course I make a point to say the word as often as I fucking can.

Benji snorts. "He wouldn't be ashamed to tell you exactly what he *is* into. Loudly. Repeatedly. In explicit detail."

I grin at him, and our eyes lock. There's a lightness in the air cutting through the tension that's stifled the two-bedroom apartment since the day I showed up without warning and ruined all of his plans.

I'm looking at him—really looking at him—for the first time.

Benji is taller than me, which isn't hard because I don't even crack five feet, but not *obscenely* tall. The right height that if he were to hug me, I'd be able to bury my face in his chest. His broad chest, thick and round, leading into a soft belly and strong legs.

He used to tease me growing up. I wouldn't go so far as to call it bullying. He would pull on my braids when he walked past me. Always hovering, he was never far away from Asher, and since Ash and I were inseparable back then…

Asher is the closest thing I have to a brother. I love him wholeheartedly. But I've never had *feelings* for him, or him for me. Our bond transcends romance and delves directly into family.

The way Benji is looking at me right now is definitely not familial. His eyes are bright, lit up with good humor. His clothes are a little rumpled, like he's been futzing with them. As I stare wordlessly at him, he shifts and tugs at his dress shirt, trying to smooth out a stubborn wrinkle. He swallows, his Adam's apple bobbing in the thick column of his throat.

Warmth spreads through me. There's a little flutter in my belly, and automatically, my hand falls to my bump. My mouth parts on a soft gasp at the unexpected sensation.

But it's not the baby. It's deeper, within me.

Benji's eyes widen. "Are you okay? Do you need anything?"

"I'm fine." My voice comes out shaky, and I reach blindly for the couch.

Asher steps forward, no doubt to help me.

Benji crosses the room in two strides. His hand settles on my upper arm as he guides me onto the sofa, nestling me among the cushions. He stares at me, his lips pursed and head tilted in thought, before he whisks the throw blanket off the back of the couch and spreads it over me.

"What are you doing?" I croak as I burrow into the thick chenille throw. Clearing my throat, I try to focus on just this singular moment. "Why are you…"

He shakes his head. "Are you okay?"

"I'm fine."

Benji purses his lips some more. "Hmm."

Asher is staring between the two of us, eyes ping-ponging back and forth like he's at a tennis match.

"Do you want some applesauce?" my roommate asks.

"I—"

He nods with authority, though I don't remember when I granted it to him.

Spinning on his heel, he strides into the kitchen and to the cupboard he designated as mine. Pulling out an applesauce pouch, he twists the top before returning to me and handing it over.

"Eat. You'll feel better."

"I feel *fine*," I tell him. Asher raises his eyebrows, and I sigh. "I swear I'm fine."

"You'll take care of her?" my best friend asks my new roommate.

"I don't need anyone to take care of me," I mutter, sucking on my applesauce pouch.

"Yes, of course," Ash says, patting me on the head.

Benji nods. "I've got her."

His eyes flick to me again, and that peculiar fluttering sensation happens again.

Okay, maybe I do need to lie down after all. I'd get up and stomp to my room, but the action kind of loses its impact when it will take me three tries to get up off the couch.

I guess I'll just stay here forever, then. I swing my legs up onto the sofa and adjust myself into a comfortable position.

To my surprise, Benji steps forward again, fluffing the blanket around me. He holds out a hand and I give him my empty pouch.

"Get some rest," he says. His voice comes out hoarse. "We'll give you space."

four

· · ·

Benji

YONI AND ELLIOTT live across town in a warm, comfortable townhouse that's the perfect size for hosting. Also, because they're the only ones that really know how to cook, all of the events are always held at their place.

Asher moved in with me after he and Elliott broke up a few years back, so even though I'm not really part of the core friend group, I'm still on the periphery. The group includes me in giant group activities, just not the smaller, more intimate get-togethers. I went to a few of Elliott's book club meetups before opting out. Those people take their book analysis *seriously*. Also, I'm not really into sci-fi and fantasy, which is where the group's interest leans.

As I help Estee out of the ride-share, my gaze automatically swoops down to her chest before I force my eyes away. At home, she's normally in oversized t-shirts and baggy sweaters. Today, she's glammed up in a burgundy wrap dress that accentuates her belly and dips low in front. Even with the help of a little white camisole beneath the dress, her curves are unmistakable.

My pregnant roommate is *hot*.

It feels wrong to lust after her.

First, there's the roommate thing. I'm offering her a safe place to stay. She doesn't need me fantasizing about her in the sanctity of her own home.

Second, there's the pregnant thing. Ash has made clear she's not with the father of the baby, but given the state of her life right now, the last thing she needs is me coming in and messing with her head.

Also, I've never gone after a pregnant woman before. I didn't think it would be something I was interested in. With the woman who becomes my wife, sure, I don't expect it to bother me—in fact, I'm thoroughly counting on her being pregnant with my child to be a massive turn-on.

When the baby isn't mine? That feels like crossing a boundary. I'm trying not to psychoanalyze myself too much or I'll head into a tailspin. It's not anything to do with the other man. *She* isn't mine. I don't look at pregnant women on the street and suddenly want them.

It's just her. I don't care whose baby Estee is carrying. I like *her*. She's single. Why can't we have a little no-strings fun?

Oh, yeah. Because I can't handle some no-strings fun with the woman I've wanted since I knew how to want.

Inside the apartment, Yoni's brother Jared opens the door and takes our coats. Automatically, I help Estee out of her jacket, and she eyes me warily but allows me to help.

"Do you know everyone?" Jared asks.

"Not really," Estee admits.

"I'll introduce you," I offer.

She flashes me a quick smile. Setting my hand on her lower back, I steer her into the living room area.

I don't know Alex and Mara well, certainly not well enough to be invited to their wedding last year, but enough that I can navigate small talk with them.

Alex claps me on the back—I cringe—and Mara gives me a perfunctory hug.

"This is Estee Cohen. Alex and Mara. Their wedding was the night Ash and Ari…"

"Oh." Her eyes go round. She's heard enough about that night.

Estee was the cause of some of their strife with some text messages that Arielle read a little too much into. She truly had no ill will toward her two oldest friends. But tone is hard to convey over text, and with everyone's emotions being heightened…

Luckily, they resolved that pretty quickly. And a year later, Arielle and Asher are engaged, so it all worked out.

"Congratulations are in order?" Alex shouts. I don't know why he's yelling.

"Huh?" It's my turn to blink at him.

Estee laughs, though it sounds forced. "We're not together," she says. "It's not his."

Mara's eyebrows go up.

"I'm friends with Arielle and Asher," she says. "Benji is offering me his spare room."

"Ohhhhh." Mara smiles. "How are you holding up?"

"Day by day," Estee says.

We chat for a few moments before Mara gets called away and we move on.

Introductions are made: Jared and Sadie. Rachel and Erik. Yoni and Elliott are busy in the kitchen, waving hello from a distance as the two of them put the finishing touches on the meal.

There are a few people from Elliott's book club. The people I don't know, Estee takes the lead, effortlessly charming them the way she's charmed me.

Asher comes barreling out of the hallway bathroom, his face red and his curls mussed. Behind him is Arielle, her dress decidedly wrinkled. It doesn't take much to put two and two together.

Estee giggles at the sight of them. "You two…" She shakes

her head in mock-exasperation. "You couldn't wait until you got home?"

Asher laughs. "Nope." He reaches for her, no doubt to give her a hug.

"No. Don't touch me with your sex hands," she teases.

He makes a show of wiping his hands on his pants before he wraps her into an enormous hug. Asher gives good hugs. That's something that hasn't changed.

Estee's whole body relaxes. Her shoulders slump as she leans into his embrace. She clings to him like she's afraid she'll be torn away from him.

"You holding up okay?" he murmurs in her ear loud enough for me to hear it.

She nods into his chest. "I'm fine."

Asher scoffs and rolls his eyes. "We talked about this."

"Yeah. We did," she says. "I'm *fine*."

"Leave it," I tell my best friend and former roommate. "She knows her own mind."

Estee pulls back, shooting me a smile. "Thanks for sticking up for me. I don't need it, though. I'm fine on my own."

Forcing a laugh, I tuck my hands into my pockets so I won't give into the urge to pull her into my side. "I know you are. Figured repetition might help get it through his thick skull."

Arielle watches me, her eyes darting between us curiously. She opens her mouth and then snaps it closed.

Shaking her head, she says, "I don't want to know."

My stomach plummets. Does that mean she doesn't want anything to happen? Or just that she doesn't want to be kept informed?

Yoni calls us to the table. Shenanigans are clearly afoot because my seat is conveniently placed next to Estee's.

Elliott sets a bowl down in front of her. It's applesauce.

"Ash told me you're having stomach issues."

Estee's eyes soften. "Thanks, El."

They give her a smile. "No problem. I want you to try the mashed potatoes, too. That might be neutral enough for you."

She gives him a watery smile. "I will."

The urge to touch her overcomes me. Slowly, so she can see my hand incoming, I reach over and squeeze her arm.

They've done nothing but welcome her into the group. I'm so happy for her. It surely is a rough transition, moving all the way from New York to Boston with no notice. And doing it pregnant, to boot. I have no idea how she does it.

Well. I do. She's not doing it well. She hides in her room, she doesn't use the common areas when I'm home. It must be lonely.

I'm going to make things more comfortable for her. Whatever it takes, I'll set her at ease.

Dinner is a loud and raucous affair. Yoni and Asher are no strangers to a good time and the handle of Tito's on the table is quickly evaporating. That doesn't include the copious amounts of moscato that Arielle, Sadie, and Mara are putting away.

Mindful that Estee can't drink, I don't imbibe, either. It hardly seems fair. I might kick back with a beer on occasion, but wine doesn't do it for me. There's enough alcohol abuse in my family history that it's scared me off indulging in hard liquor too much; the second I start itching for a drink, I know it's time to back off again.

She's quiet. I don't know how much is her natural personality and how much is emotional overwhelm. I haven't known her—really, truly known her—since we were kids.

Who is Estee Cohen?

She's a grown woman, not the young girl I used to tease. She's lived an entire life since we knew each other.

five

. . .

Estee

IF BENJI DOESN'T STOP HOVERING, I'm going to fucking scream.

It started when Asher came to the house, but in the week since Thanksgiving, it's ramped up. He's always *there*—watching, waiting.

For what? For me to mess up more? For him to gloat?

He's not the same bratty kid who used to tease me. I can even buy he's genuinely concerned for me.

Why? Because my entire life is up in flames? I'm doing just fine, thank you very much.

Because of the long weekend, he was home with nothing to do, so I stayed in my room to give him space.

If I spend one more fucking minute alone in my room, I'm going to end up back in the psych ward. I know there's a difference between isolation and seeking solitude, and I'm toeing the line now, but I don't know how to do this when I don't feel comfortable in this apartment.

Tip-toeing into the main room, I'm surprised to find it empty.

I'm hiding away and he isn't even fucking *here*?

Making my way to the kitchen, I grab an applesauce pouch and am assaulted by the most delicious scent. There's a big pan on the stove, sauce bubbling around cabbage leaves stuffed with the most tantalizing meat mixture.

Footsteps clomp behind me. Caught, I whirl to face Benji.

"You're alive," he says dryly. His warm eyes take their time in caressing my body. "How are you feeling?"

"Hungry," I admit.

"Good thing we have food," he says, giving me a small smile.

Swallowing, I gather my courage. "Are you making stuffed cabbage?"

Guarded, he nods. "Is the smell too strong?"

"No. Fuck no," I tell him quickly. "It smells so good. Is it ready yet?"

He checks his watch. "In about half an hour."

My stomach plummets. "Oh."

"You can hang out with me while it cooks," he offers. "You don't have to stay locked up in your room."

I hesitate.

"No pressure. I want you to be comfortable here. Really."

Squinting at him, I try to give him the benefit of the doubt. "What do you get out of it?"

"I get an awesome roommate to hang out with," Benji says with a shrug. "If you don't want to be friends, we don't have to. No skin off my back."

"I… I guess I can wait half an hour," I say slowly. I grab an applesauce pouch to tide me over. I can't guarantee the spice of the stuffed cabbage won't make me sick, but right now, it smells so good that I can't care.

The enormous smile that stretches across his face lights up his features. Whereas before I thought he was good-looking, now he's downright gorgeous.

Since he's been home all last weekend, he skipped shaving

the last few days, and he didn't shave for work this week, so there's a light layer of stubble covering his face. His black t-shirt stretches across his broad chest and soft belly. And those gray sweatpants? They should be *illegal.*

My stomach flutters and my hand automatically goes to my bump.

"Are you okay?" Benji asks immediately. He starts toward me, his arms outstretched.

But it's not the baby. It's *me.*

Benji is fucking hot. The pregnancy hormones have been driving me nuts. I'm not just hiding away in my room; my toy collection is getting a solid workout, too.

My ex didn't want to have sex once I started showing. It freaked him out. It's not like he didn't know exactly how I got knocked up. Once it was real for him, once he could see it with his own eyes, he lost all interest in me.

I like toys, don't get me wrong. I have an extensive collection for a reason. There's a time and place for them in the bedroom, and I especially like using them *with* my partner.

But there's nothing like the smooth slide of a hard, hot cock thrusting into me. The heat of a man surrounding me, his scent enveloping me. And then after? Curling up together, sweaty and sated? It can't be beat.

"Are you okay?" Benji asks again.

How do I ask my super hot roommate to fuck me silly? Can I even ask that? Will it ruin everything?

"I'm fine." The words come out breathy and I cringe. Fuck. I'm not trying to come onto him.

"You're red. And kind of sweaty."

I make a face. Great. He probably thinks I'm the grossest person in the world.

"Pregnancy hormones." Taking a step back, I make my way to the sofa and ease myself down, curling my leg beneath me.

To my surprise, Benji takes the seat on the other end and folds a leg up, too.

"That must be difficult," he says. "Feeling like you're not in control." He shakes his head. "I don't know that I could do it."

"Well, luckily, you don't have the anatomy for it." My tone is this side of bitter.

"I already have enough out-of-body experiences," he continues, ignoring my tone.

"Oh?"

He chews his cheek. "Did Ash tell you I have OCD?"

"Not really. He just said you were kind of a neat freak."

Benji snorts. "That's one way to put it. I was hospitalized after a particularly bad episode." When I don't say anything, he hurries to add: "I'm in a good place now. I take my meds, I have regular therapy, I'm doing well."

Shifting uncomfortably, it's my turn to share my secrets:

"I spent three weeks in the psych ward when I was in law school." I swallow. "Depressive episode. I'm medicated also."

They had to change my dosage when I got pregnant unexpectedly, as my prior meds weren't pregnancy-safe. I'm not always sure they're working these days.

"So we have something in common." He gives me a crooked smile. "There, it's not so hard, is it?"

"What?"

"Opening up. Hanging out."

Shaking my head, I laugh a little. "I don't know, I don't normally share that story with people."

"I'm not people," Benji says quietly. "I've been there, I've gone through it. Maybe mine presented differently, but it's the same principle. The mental health struggle."

I sigh. "And some days, it's more of a struggle than others."

"How are you doing? Really?"

His eyes are open, nonjudgmental. I truly believe he wants to know.

"Some days are better than others. I don't know how to do this alone," I admit.

Benji waits patiently.

"When I got pregnant, I was so excited. You know? We were engaged, we're having a baby, it's like it was all coming together." My stomach curls around my bump.

Letting out a cold laugh, I shake my head. "So much has changed. I'm not the same person I was six months ago or even six weeks ago."

"But do you like the person you are now?" he asks quietly.

I take the time to consider.

"I want to. I miss feeling like *me*."

"What can I do to help you feel like yourself?"

"It's not your burden to bear."

Benji frowns. "I want it to be, though."

I swallow the lump in my throat. "What does that mean?"

"We're friends. Right?"

He waits for me to nod, and when I do, he smiles.

"Friendship means looking out for one another. Making sure we're in a happy, healthy place."

"I want to be there," I admit. "I just don't know how to get there."

He chews his lip. "Would it help to do things you enjoy? What are your hobbies?"

"I like to work."

He laughs. "Yeah, you and everyone else in our generation, we're all workaholics. What else?"

"In general, I like to do outdoorsy things. In the winter…" I sigh. "It's hard. I know I probably *can* do some of the things, but I'm nervous. My center of gravity is off."

The temperature is hovering just above freezing. If the slick covering the ground turns to ice, I'm risking more than just myself: I'm risking my gremlin, too.

"Do you watch TV? Read?" Benji asks guilelessly.

"I like to watch hockey," I finally say.

"Hawks fan?"

I make a face. "No way. Grizzlies all the way."

"Really? Even living in New York?"

"I was a transplant, I've only lived there for a year and a half. Not enough to form an allegiance to any of their shitty sports teams."

Benji laughs loudly. "Okay, tell it like you see it."

"I'm a Grizzlies fan because of Ash. He's such a big fan. When I was in law school, he'd come to LA whenever the Grizzlies had a game in town and we'd go." I shake my head. "Or last year, he came up to New York for the game."

"Baseball? The Sox?"

"Meh. They're okay." I shrug. "I'll watch in season in the background, but really only to support Arielle. Before she signed with the team, I didn't watch baseball at all. And don't get me started on basketball. Gag."

He huffs out a soft breath of laughter. "Football?"

"Go Blue." I give him a toothy smile. I did my undergrad at Michigan before heading to UCLA for law school. I bleed maize and blue.

He went to Penn State, I know, because Asher mentioned it, like, fourteen times over the last few years they lived together. Ash went to Indiana. We're all Big 10 rivals.

"The Chicago football team has been trash for the last seventeen years," I add on. "I'll watch it if it's on, but I don't go out of my way to seek it out."

"Hmm." Benji pulls his phone from his pocket, flicking through it, and I take that as a signal the conversation is over.

A timer goes off on the stove, and he lurches to his feet before loping his way to the kitchen. He turns off the timer and then lifts the lid off the pan.

The enticing scent of tomato sauce, boiled cabbage, and spiced meat fills the small apartment. Even from my position on the couch, I can smell it so clearly I can almost taste it. My mouth waters. I think I let out a moan. I bury my face in my hands. Did anyone else hear that, or was it just me?

He bustles through the kitchen, doing stuff that I can't see, so I'm surprised when he comes to stand in front of me, a bowl in his hand.

"Here," Benji says, thrusting the bowl into my hand. "Careful, it's hot."

I blink up at him. "I can't eat this."

"Too much?"

"It's yours."

He shakes his head. "I want you to eat it. To enjoy it."

"If you insist…"

I take the bowl and the fork he gives me. As I cut into one of the stuffed cabbage rolls, it practically falls apart, steam billowing up to punch me in the face with flavor.

"What made you decide to make it?" I ask as I let it cool a bit.

"First freeze of the year." He shrugs. "I normally like to stock up the freezer a bit when it gets cold out. With holiday parties and things on the calendar, I don't always have enough time to cook."

My stomach turns. "I can't—"

"I want you to have some," he says firmly. "Fuck, eat all of it, I don't care. I want you to eat."

I open my mouth to protest, but my stomach grumbles. Evidently, the applesauce earlier wasn't enough.

"I know you have nausea issues. It sucks, I feel for you," he adds. "It would bring me great joy for you to eat my food."

Shamefaced, I look away.

A fingertip beneath my chin forces my eyes up to his.

"I want you to take care of yourself," Benji says quietly. "No more hiding."

"I won't."

"Promise?" He gives me what I think is meant to be a

cheeky grin, but there's a heaviness in his eyes and serious-
ness in his tone that gives me pause.

"I do," I tell him.

He mutters something under his breath.

It almost sounds like he said *I wish*.

six

. . .

Benji

CHANUKAH IS FAST APPROACHING. I don't know what I should get for Estee. I know we're not gift-giving friends yet, but it feels like something I *should* do.

"Riv," I ask over a morning coffee break. "What sort of gift would you want from your weirdo roommate if you were seven months pregnant, unexpectedly single, and have no real place to go?"

My coworker glares at me. "I'm going to ignore the weirdo part and dive straight into the pregnant, alone, and definitely doesn't want her roommate hitting on her part."

I sigh. Yeah, that's what I was afraid of.

"I just want to do something *nice* for her. She doesn't have anyone looking out for her."

She narrows her eyes. "Maybe she could look out for herself."

"Oh, I know she can *take care* of herself. She's strong and independent and I admire her for that," I add quickly. "Everyone needs someone to look out for them. I'm not trying to stop her from living her life. I just want to protect her."

Riv shakes her head. "You're an idiot, Benji."

"Well, yeah, I know *that*." My parents tell me often

enough. "I like her. I'm not trying to pursue her romantically, I know she's not in the headspace for that. But I like her. I want to do something nice for her."

Chet pokes his head up from his desk. I thought he was ignoring us, his enormous headphones over his ears.

"Pamper her. Treat her to a spa day," he says. "Do the sort of things you'd do if she was knocked up with your kid. You guys aren't a couple, but she's still your friend. She's more than an incubator. She's a person with needs and wants, too. Figure out what they are and problem-solve her a gift that way."

I blink at him a few times. "Who the hell *are* you?"

Chet blushes. "I'm just… I'm me. Who the hell are you?"

Riv shakes her head. "You idiots are ridiculous."

After work, I head to the shopping center a few blocks away. There has to be something that is worthy enough of Estee. I don't want anything generic. A gift isn't worth mentioning if it isn't from the heart.

There's a massage place that offers subscriptions. I don't know if she's going to want a recurring massage.

They do offer prenatal massages, as well as postpartum. I didn't know what those two words meant until last week, now I'm well-versed. I've been reading *What to Expect When You're Expecting* on my Kindle.

Leaving the store with two gift certificates in hand, I catch a scent in the air. Following my nose, I find myself walking into a bath supplies store. They have every kind of soap and scent I can think of.

"Looking for something specific?" The sales clerk is a perky young woman with turquoise hair and a ring through her nose.

"I just—I smelled…"

"What kind of scent?" she asks.

I shrug. "I'm not sure. It was—it smells like her."

"Your girlfriend?" she prompts.

"Roommate." I clear my throat. "I want to get something for her."

"What does she like?"

"She's very sensitive to scents," I finally say. "She wears a subtle gardenia perfume, but I don't know what she'd enjoy. We're just friends."

The clerk gives me a knowing smile. "We have a variety of floral products."

She leads me over to the wall, which is covered floor to ceiling in fancy bath soaps and gels.

"I want—she likes…" She has a shower in her bathroom, but mine has a tub with the fancy jets. "Bubble bath."

"Right then." The clerk points at a few products. "This is the one I'd recommend. You can smell it now and see if you like it."

"It's not for me. It's for her."

She smirks at me. "The scent will fill your home. You have to like it, too."

Opening the first bottle, a vanilla and rose concoction, the cloying sweetness punches me in the gut.

"Nope. Not this."

Handing it back, she offers me another bottle.

This one is more subtle, woodsy and a hint of spice. Cinnamon, maybe.

"She's not a forest," I decide, handing it back. "It smells nice, but… no."

On the third try, she nails it.

There's an undercurrent of coffee in the vanilla. It reminds me of curling up on the sofa with a good book, hot cocoa, and a heavy blanket.

Hmm… maybe that's what I can do for Estee.

By the time I get home, there's a pep in my step that even the bone-chilling wind can't erase. I'm going to do this. I'm going to be her friend. I'm going to take care of her.

However she'll let me.

seven

. . .

Benji

ESTEE IS ON THE COUCH, wearing an oversized sweater and leggings, her feet bare. She looks over at me and offers a small smile.

"Hey. How was work?"

"Good." I hang up my coat. What do I do with the present? Do I hide it? Do I just hand it to her?

She struggles to get off the couch, a blanket across her shoulders. "I'm going to make dinner. What are you in the mood for?"

"Actually…" I catch her arm as she walks by me. "Do you mind if we light the menorah together?"

Estee blinks a few times. "What?"

"It's the first night of Chanukah. I like to light the candles." I scratch at my cheek, where the stubble is growing in itchy.

I'm not religious, but there are some cultural traditions I like to maintain. Lighting the candles is one of them.

"Yeah," Estee says, giving me a smile. "I'd like that, too."

The menorah is kept in a box above the fridge with all of my other Judaica. I'm not sure why I keep it there, really, except lack of anywhere better. I don't light the Shabbat candles each week, and Chanukah is only one week a year, so it doesn't make sense to use up prime real estate with it. My parents have a china hutch where they display theirs—they also don't light the Shabbat candles regularly—but I don't feel like I'm in a place in my life where I need a china hutch.

Maybe when I get married.

Maybe not even then. I don't know if we'll be the sort of couple who needs "fancy" dishes.

Then again… there's no "we."

No matter how much I want there to be.

Estee comes to stand beside me, her fingertips brushing over the sleek marble and metal menorah. It was a gift from a person I'm no longer in touch with; she bought it in Israel and brought it home for me. I dumped her but kept the menorah. I like it.

She adds the two candles: one for the night's celebrations, and the Shamash, the leading candle. I offer her the matchbox and she lights the candle, using the Shamash to light the far right candle.

Taking her hand, I interlock our fingers as we say the two Chanukah blessings, plus the Schehechiyanu, the special blessing said on the first night of Chanukah and at the start of something new.

Because it is. This is something new.

Estee looks down at our entwined fingers, a strange look on her face. She doesn't pull away, though.

There's no need to hold hands while saying the blessings. It just felt right.

Clearing my throat, I announce: "I got you something."

Her eyes widen. "Oh. I didn't know…"

I shake my head. "I saw it and thought of you."

Pulling out the gift bag, I watch as she pulls out a bottle of bubble bath, some epsom salts, a bottle of scented lotion, and a pair of fuzzy socks.

"There's something else," I add, when she stops.

"Benji, this is… it's a lot."

Reaching into the bag, I hand her the envelope. "I thought you might like a massage."

"Oh, I don't know…"

"They specialize in prenatal massage," I tell her, showing her the gift certificate. "There's also a coupon for one after the baby's born."

To my surprise, her eyes well with tears.

"Oh. Shit. No." I recoil. "Please don't cry. I don't want to upset you."

Estee shakes her head, swiping at her eyes. "You're not upsetting me. You're being kind to me."

"Well, yeah. That's what friends do."

She swallows, then looks up at me. "Is that what we are? Friends?"

My throat seizes. "I'd like to think so, yeah."

Would I kill to be more? Yes, absolutely. But I also recognize she's not in a headspace where she can really feel comfortable acting on it.

"I, um. I don't have a bathtub." Her bathroom only has a shower.

"I do. It has jets." I pause. "Will the jets hurt the baby?"

"They shouldn't," she says. "I can't use your bathtub, though."

"You can and you will."

"But—"

"I'll draw you a bath and you can relax while I prep dinner," I announce.

Estee opens her mouth and then closes it. "Okay," she finally says.

Heading into the bathroom, I start the water and add some of the bubbles before changing out of my work clothes. My room is mostly picked up, my bed haphazardly made, my sex toys hidden away. Looks good enough for company.

Not *company*. Nobody else is going to share my bed. But she'll *see* it, and that's enough to make me self-conscious.

Heading back into the main living area in a t-shirt and sweatpants, I find her standing in front of the candles, looking down at them wistfully.

"Bath's ready," I tell her.

"Thanks," she says, her voice quiet.

"I'll get started on dinner."

"Do we have any more stuffed cabbage?" Her eyes dart between me, the candles, and the fridge.

"I think so," I say around a smile. "Would you like some?"

She nods, looking like she wants to say something. I wait patiently.

But there are no more words.

She turns around and heads toward my door, closing the bathroom door with a soft *snick*. A few moments later, there's a splash like she's entered the tub.

Fuck. My cock reacts to the thought of her naked in my tub, covered in nothing but a thin layer of bubbles. Estee Cohen is naked in my bathroom.

And I'm stuck in the living room, pining after her like a schmuck.

Puttering around the kitchen, I pull out dishes and plates. As much as she might like to, we can't live off stuffed cabbage alone. It's got meat and rice and sauce, but not a lot of other nutrients. I steam some peas and carrots to go along with it and throw together a quick salad.

"Benji?" Estee's voice calls from the other room.

I drop what I'm doing and race to her, stopping outside the closed bathroom door. "What's wrong?"

"You can open the door," she says.

Cracking it open, I poke my head in. The tub is deep enough that she can sit properly, and the water comes up to the tops of her breasts, bubbles obscuring her tantalizing flesh.

"I'm hungry," she announces.

Shaking my head, I have to smile as I ask, "do you want to eat your stuffed cabbage in the tub?"

"I do, actually," she says. "Is that okay?"

"Yeah, that's fine." My belly warms at the idea of her eating my food. "I'll be right back."

Quickly, I prepare her a bowl—a plate will *not* work in this scenario—with the peas and carrots serving as a bed for two stuffed cabbage rolls. I even take the time to cut it up into smaller chunks so she won't need to use the knife while in the tub.

Once it's heated through, I pour a bit of sparkling apple juice into a wine glass and grab the bowl.

Estee's pulled her dark hair onto her head. With it piled up into a bun, I can see the purple streaks running through it. The dye is fading, grown out.

"Oh, I could kiss you right now," she announces as I deliver the bowl. She sits up a little more and the water sloshes in the tub.

I'm careful to keep my eyes on her face. "Enjoy your dinner."

"Wait," she says, when I reach the doorframe.

"Everything okay?" I look at her over my shoulder, because if I turn around right now, I might just launch myself at her.

"Stay."

I blink.

"Sit with me," Estee says quietly. She looks away. "I mean..."

"You're okay if I stay?"

"I want you to stay," she insists. "I just... I'm alone all day, and I'm alone all night, and I... I don't want to be alone."

My heart breaks for her. "I'll stay," I decide.

The apartment is pretty large by Boston standards, but it's not enormous. I curl up with my back to the door, perpendicular to the tub, as she splashes in the tub and eats her stuffed cabbage.

The high sides of the tub keep me from seeing anything, and even if they didn't, the bubbles offer her a modicum of privacy.

Still, I am uncomfortably aware of the fact that she is *naked*. In my tub. Her clothes—folded neatly on the closed toilet lid—are a stark reminder that the power imbalance skews mightily in my favor.

"How was your day?" I ask casually, running a hand over my chin. I skipped shaving this morning and it's starting to itch. I prefer the way my face looks clean-shaven. It's too easy for a full beard to look unkempt with my curly hair, and the three-day-old stubble look just makes me look hungover.

"It was good. Another fun day of contract law." Estee shakes her head, a smile twisting her lips. "I need to look for something new, but searching for a new job while pregnant isn't exactly easy, and then I might not be eligible for leave… My current job sucks, yeah, but at least I get a decent maternity leave package."

"Are you going to go back to work after the baby's born?"

"I'll need to, won't I? I've got bills to pay. Shit, I have to find an apartment." She chews on her lip.

"Don't worry about that," I tell her. "You're staying here."

"For now, yeah."

"For now," I agree. "I'd like for you to stay here once the baby's born."

Estee laughs. "You can't be serious."

"Look, you won't be working, you'll be on your own, and I have the space." I scratch at my chin. "I'd like for you to stay."

"You want me to stay here with a newborn? What if you want to bring a date home?"

"So I'll go back to her place," I shrug. "Trust me, I don't go out much."

She mutters something under her breath.

"I wouldn't feel comfortable with you moving out with a newborn. Seriously, I'd like you to stay—for as long as you'd like to stay."

"I can't pay you much…"

"Keep paying for groceries and you can stay forever," I joke. It's time to come clean. I exhale slowly. "Look, the apartment isn't much, but it's free rent and you can save up. I'll cover the utilities, you have the groceries, and we're good."

Estee narrows her eyes at me. "How did you get such a cheap rent?"

I shrug. "My grandparents left it to me in their will. The mortgage is dirt cheap—like, I'm tempted to pay it off altogether because the balance is so low, but the monthly rate is good, so it doesn't make financial sense."

"So what you're saying is I need rich grandparents," she muses slowly.

"Average grandparents who died," I correct.

She flinches. "Sorry. Forgot about that part."

I shrug. "It was a while ago. But when I moved here for grad school, it was a good place to live, and since I pay the bills on my salary, I don't have to worry about a renter."

"But Asher lived here."

"Because he needed a place to stay. I like Ash." Even if he does have a penchant for noisy sex. "I'd rather it be someone I know and like than a stranger. And I know you and I like you."

I like her a lot.

Estee hums around a bite of stuffed cabbage.

Fuck. Why is that so adorable?

She finishes her bowl and I take it from her, setting it on the ground beside the tub. Bringing her hands inside the tub, she dunks them beneath the water and then draws them over her arms, spreading the warm water over her shoulders.

Estee sighs happily. "This is the life."

"Well, you can use my bathtub any time," I tell her.

And it's true. She can. With an ordinary roommate, I'd be more concerned about them being all up in my space.

With her? She can have anything she wants from me. Hell, I'd even give her my last name.

eight

. . .

Estee

I WANT to do something nice for Benji. I just don't know what to *do*.

He's been so kind to me, nothing like the loud-mouthed kid I remember. He seems to genuinely care about me and my feelings. And he's letting me stay in his apartment virtually rent-free!

Since it's the weekend, he's home, and I can hear him puttering around the kitchen. I don't have the strength to go out and approach him. What do I even say? *Thanks for sitting on the bathroom floor while I was naked in your tub?*

Rubbing at my eyes, I try to focus. What do I get him? I'll have to go out to the shops; I can't just order it for delivery and expect it right away. I think about texting Asher for help before I decide against it. I can do this on my own.

I can do hard things. I can do anything I set my mind to.

When I hear his door *snick* shut, I leave mine. I grab a quick brunch of yogurt and granola before I pull on my coat and leave. I don't know where I'm going, just that it isn't here.

It's bitterly cold, but the air is crisp and clear, no snow or ice on the horizon. I wrap my scarf around my neck and burrow into my coat. The subway—no, the *T*, I correct myself, I live in Boston now—is fairly crowded. People have shopping bags. More people are wearing Grizzlies jerseys. Given the size of the crowd heading into downtown, I'm guessing there's a game today.

I don't know where to go or what I want to do, so I find myself heading into the downtown area, too. Following the crowd, I exit at the hockey arena, and my feet pull me in the direction of the ticket counter.

I was right; there is a game tonight against the Habs. Tickets are sold out.

Instead, I pick a random game next month and buy two tickets for that.

I don't have any Grizzlies gear; I'll have to fix that. When I enter the pro shop, I'm drawn to a black and gold hoodie with the team's logo on front and Lewis on the nameplate. Jake Lewis is a Jewish hockey player on the Grizzlies, a goalie, and he's damn good at it. I'd be proud to wear his name on my back.

Picking up a hoodie, I make sure to get a size that will fit over my growing bump before heading toward the men's section. Would Benji be okay wearing another man's name on his back? I'm genuinely not sure. I don't understand why he *wouldn't* be, but fragile masculinity doesn't make sense to me, either.

Not that I think Benji's sense of self is all that fragile. He seems down to earth and easygoing. Then again, I thought that about my ex, and he was a shining example that what you see isn't always what you get.

Bypassing the issue entirely, I grab a hoodie with a grizzly bear and the Centennial logo on it. It's kind of cool that this year is the hockey club's one hundred year anniversary.

When I make it back to the apartment, I'm immediately assaulted by the scent of roasting meat.

Normally, that is not a scent I'd enjoy. Especially lately, it's enough to turn my stomach at the mere thought of it.

But when I see Benji standing at the kitchen island, wearing a leather and canvas apron and carving a roast, my stomach flips.

"What are you doing?" I demand.

He looks up and grins at me. His entire face lights up. "Hey. Did you have a good day?"

I cross my arms over my chest, wincing at my sore breasts. "What are you making?"

"I made a brisket and carrot tzimmes," he says, continuing to slice the meat. "I'll make latkes later, too."

"Who are you?!"

He laughs, a little nervous. "I'm just me."

Dropping my bags, I move to the kitchen island, peeking into the roasting pan. "Do you make a sweet or savory brisket?"

"Sweet. From the Hadassah *Noodles and Strudels* cookbook," he says. "I've modified it to not need corn syrup, though."

"I could kiss you," I declare.

Benji chuckles nervously. "Okay?"

"It looks absolutely delicious."

The brisket is on the cutting board, leaving the pan chock-full of carrots, potatoes, and onions covered in a brown sugar glaze.

My mother's brisket is a savory tomato-based brisket. It's *fine*. There's nothing wrong with it. We spent most holidays with Asher's family, and they make a sweet brisket. In fact, I'm fairly certain that's the recipe Benji's using.

Hadassah is an international women's organization, similar to gentile Ladies' Aid. And in the 70s, the Beverly Hills chapter of Hadassah put together a cookbook called *From Noodles to Strudels*. The book with the lime green cover was a staple in our house. More than half of our classic family recipes came from this cookbook.

The brisket recipe itself is simple, just time consuming. There's no word as to the author or creator of the recipe. Whoever they were, they did the world a service by sharing this brisket recipe.

Benji slices the meat, then stabs a piece with the tip of the knife and holds it out to me. "Taste?"

I don't second guess it. I pluck the roasted beef off the knife and gobble it down. My eyes fall closed at the sweet, salty, and rich flavor of the meat. It tastes like home. Cozy.

"Do you only cook Jewish food?" I ask, half joking.

He laughs outright, shaking his head. "No. I've just been in the mood lately. I think I'm nesting."

I blink. "You're nesting?"

"It's getting cold and snowy. Time to nest," he declares. "I don't mind going out, but if I can stay at home and curl up on the couch, I'd rather do that."

"There's a hockey game on soon. Do you… would you like to watch? Together?"

Benji smiles from ear to ear. "I'd like that."

Once he finishes slicing the meat, he puts the roasting pan back in the oven and washes his hands.

"What did you get up to today?" he asks with a smile.

"Oh. Um…"

"You don't have to tell me," he says. Reaching across the island, he squeezes my arm. "You deserve your privacy."

"I got us tickets to the Grizzlies," I blurt.

It's his turn to blink.

"The game is early January. I thought it might be something fun to do together."

He exhales heavily. "Yeah, that sounds great," he says, his eyes bright. "I'd love that."

It's still early, so I head to my room to take a late afternoon nap. I'm tired, like, all the time. And sweaty. And horny. My body is changing so much, sometimes by the day, and I feel like I'm being possessed half the time. I don't feel like myself.

I want to love this little gremlin. I want us to have a good life. But sometimes I don't know what that's going to look like. What kind of life can I give them? A single, unmarried mother who works all the time, alone in a new city with no place to go…

Benji offered for me—us—to stay, but he can't mean that, not really. I'm sure as soon as the baby's born, he'll come up with an excuse for us to leave. No single man wants to play house with a baby that isn't his. Hell, even if the baby *were* his, there's still a chance he'd not want to be part of our lives. It's not that far of a reach.

He doesn't seem like the type, though. I don't see him walking away from his kid. Hypothetically, that is. He's not like my ex. He's an actual nice person.

… And *there* are my blinders. I'm thinking of Benji as if I know him. I don't. We went to summer camp together when we were kids and only recently fell back into one another's lives. I don't know him as a person. Not really.

I want to, though.

nine

. . .

Benji

WHEN ESTEE COMES out of her room, she's glowing. Her hair is wet and loose around her shoulders, the subtle waves framing her face. She's wearing an oversized wool sweater that falls off her shoulder and fuzzy socks on her feet.

The socks I gave her last night.

There's a crack in front of me, a sizzle and a pop, and I turn my attention back to the latkes I'm frying. The traditional potato pancakes are eaten at Chanukah so, even though I personally hate frying anything, I dug out the heavy cast iron pan to give her the feast she deserves.

"Are you making latkes?" she asks, sitting at the kitchen island a safe distance away.

Nodding, I flip one of the potato clusters, showing off the golden brown coloring. "The scent doesn't bother you?"

She hums. "Not yet."

I'll take that as a good thing, then.

As I fry up the batch of latkes, a comfortable silence wraps around us. She has her cheek propped by her fist as she watches me work. I kind of like it. It's soothing, having her here with me. Even when we aren't talking, I never feel like I need to work to fill the silence. We can simply exist.

There aren't a lot of people I feel that way with. Asher, maybe. My sister. Definitely not my parents.

When the five pounds of potatoes and onions are fried up, I turn off the pan and assemble the platter. The brisket gets pulled from the oven, too. I made a simple roasted asparagus for a little greenery to cut the heavy meal.

Estee licks her lips. "You really went all out."

I shrug. "I was bored."

She stares at me. "You were *bored*?"

I mean, I also wanted to do this. For her. She needs a community, a safe place to come home to.

I want to be that for her.

Together, we light the Chanukah candles and say the blessings. Again, I find her hand in mine. Did I grab hers? Or did she reach for me?

Either way, I squeeze her hand lightly before I release her, and reach for a plate. Handing it to her, she sighs happily as she serves herself brisket, potatoes, and carrots, then goes for the latkes. I even got cinnamon applesauce in a jar rather than her pouches for the occasion.

Once she's settled, I fill a plate for myself as well. There's nothing like laboring in a hot kitchen all day to sit down with a meal prepared with love.

Sitting side by side at the kitchen island, we chat as we eat our dinner. She tells me about a contract she wrapped up yesterday and I talk about a work thing I have to go to tomorrow.

"It's nice that you have coworkers nearby," she says. "I wish I had that."

"You want to go into the office?" Her company's head-quarters are in the Midwest somewhere.

"It would be nice. Not all the time," she adds quickly. "Just every once in a while."

"We have a conference room nobody uses. I can see if they'll let you borrow it," I offer.

"Oh, I could never…" Estee shakes her head.

I clear my throat. "Do you want to go to the holiday party?"

She blinks at me.

"It's downtown at this bougie bar," I continue. "Attendance is pretty much mandatory. I tried to explain that a holiday party on a Sunday night wasn't the best timing, but they overruled me. So. I have to go."

Estee swallows. "And you want me to go with you?"

"It might be fun." My palms sweat and my heart races. I hope she can't tell. "Might be nice to get out of the house for a bit, be with other grown-ups."

She smirks. "Are you not a grown-up?"

"I can be." I can be anything she wants me to be.

"I'll think about it," she finally says.

We clean up the dinner dishes side by side. After, we move to the couch in time for the Grizzlies game. Oh, they're playing Montreal. That'll be a nice matchup.

Estee starts out at the other end of the couch. I toss the throw blanket over her lap and she smiles up at me. Her hair is mostly dry now, the dark waves turning into curls as they dry. I smile when I see the strands of purple peeking through.

Her feet are only inches from my leg. Before I can second guess it, I lift her feet and scoot over, so her ankles are across my lap.

She goes tense.

"What are you doing?" Her voice shakes.

Picking up one foot, I rub the arch over the cozy material of the fuzzy sock. She shudders.

"You're spoiling me," she complains.

"Good. You deserve to be spoiled," I counter, continuing with the foot massage.

"I got you a present," she says.

"I don't need a present."

"I know. I wanted to get you one, anyways." She points at

the corner, where there's a Grizzlies carrier bag. "I got us both hoodies to wear to the game."

My chest gets all achy and itchy. I scratch at my collarbone but it doesn't fade away. Fuck.

"Thank you," I tell her sincerely. "I love it."

"You haven't even seen it," Estee huffs.

"It's from you. I already love it."

Her cheeks pink and she looks away.

We let the game distract us for a bit. I continue to massage her feet. If the sighs and soft moans falling from her lips are any indication, she needed this, whether she knew it or not.

Halfway through the first period, Estee swings her feet off my lap. I let her go without complaint, even though I'm dying inside at the loss of her.

But then she shifts on the couch to curl up beside me. She sets her head on my shoulder and wraps her arm around my torso.

"This okay?" she murmurs into my chest.

It's perfect. I wrap my arm around her shoulder and pull the blanket over our laps.

After that? My concentration is shot. I can't focus on the game. All I can think about is her light gardenia perfume and the floral scent of her shampoo. Her swollen belly presses against my side.

I draw my hand up and down her arm, memorizing the feeling of her. I could do this forever.

When she shifts for the third time in two minutes, I pull back a little.

"Are you okay?"

"Just uncomfortable. I have a knot in my shoulder." She grimaces. "I need to call that massage place. Thank you, by the way. I appreciate it."

I don't tell her I'd do anything for her.

"Why don't you sit on the floor and I give you a back rub?" I say instead.

Estee's eyebrows go up. "A back rub?"

My cheeks heat. "Yeah?"

"That isn't code for something else?" She smirks at me.

"Your back is hurting. We're here. I can try to help until you can get in for the massage."

She blows out a breath and scoots down to the floor. I set my feet on either side of her hips, bracketing her in.

"Where does it hurt?"

She points to her shoulder blade. "I can't get it out. I tried foam rolling and I think I made it worse."

"I'm no massage therapist, but if it starts to hurt, you let me know and I'll stop."

Estee turns her head to look at me. "Do I need a safe word?" she deadpans.

"I mean, couldn't hurt." I feel like an absolute tool when I wink at her, but she smiles and her eyes go bright.

"Ketchup," she says.

"Ketchup?"

"Hate it. Doesn't belong on this planet," she says vehemently.

"Got it. Ketchup it is."

Reverently, I run my hand over her hair and then pull it over her other shoulder. Her sweater has slipped down, revealing part of her shoulders, too.

"Here. This might help," Estee says, before she whips off her sweater.

She's wearing a thin tank top beneath, and with my positioning behind her on the couch, I have a direct line of sight down her shirt. Her breasts are just *there*, on display.

Fuck. What did I get myself into?

Still, if I'm going to hell, I might as well make it worth it. I start to massage her back, paying extra attention to the tension in her shoulder. She's loose and limber in front of me, relaxed. She sags against me, her head on my knee, her hand wrapped around my ankle like she needs something to hold onto.

It takes half the first period and most of the first intermission before she's able to find some relief. She lets out a loud, low groan that goes straight to my aching cock before she slumps against my leg.

"That's it," she says, her voice hoarse. "That's the spot."

I don't let up; I keep going, digging into the troublesome knot until it releases.

"I think I can die now," she says, sounding drugged.

That brings everything into sharp clarity for me. "What?"

Estee turns to face me. "Happy. I can die happy, now."

Pressing a hand to my chest, I try to calm my racing heart. "You don't get to die on me. No dying allowed."

"Aye, aye, cap'n," she says, offering me a salute.

It takes her two tries to get off the floor, even with my hand helping her up, and then she immediately drops down beside me. She burrows into me, her arm around me again.

"Thanks for that," she says to my chest.

"Anytime." I bring my arm down to hold her, breathing her in. There's a faint poke in my side and I twitch slightly. And then it happens again. Huh.

Estee brings a hand up to her belly, rubbing over the swell. Because I haven't replaced the blanket yet, I can see movement there.

"Is that…?"

She looks up at me, confused. "Do you need me to cover up?"

I shake my head. "Can I feel?"

She blinks at me. "You want to touch my belly?"

My face heats. "Never mind. That's weird."

She grabs my hand and brings it to her swollen bump. Over the thin cotton tank top, her skin is warm and firm.

"Say something," she says. "The baby likes your voice."

"It does? How do you know?"

There's movement beneath my palm, a little flutter.

"Was that…?"

"That's the baby," Estee says. "They're kicking."

I've never felt something like this. It's like the entire world zeroes in on this moment, this miracle that she's bringing into this world.

I care about Estee, that's for sure. I have feelings for her.

But her baby? I'm already in love with them.

I focus on the here and now. "You don't know if it's a boy or a girl?"

She shakes her head. "I want to be surprised." She sighs, shaking her head. "Well, really, I don't want people to try to assign arbitrary gender roles to a little bitty thing. And I know that if I find out, I won't be able to stop telling people. So I'm not finding out, and once the baby's born, they'll be in gender neutral clothes, and I can tell people that asking about what genitals are in a child's diaper is invasive, and hopefully I can kick some bigoted ass at the same time."

A smile shapes my lips. "You would be great at it."

A firm punch beneath my palm punctuates my words.

She bites her lip.

"What?" I ask, giving in to the urge to tuck one of her loose curls behind her ear. Her hair is just as soft as I imagined.

"So, um…" She laughs nervously. "You gave me a foot massage."

My eyebrows go up. "I did."

"And you rubbed my back."

Swallowing hard, I nod. "I did."

"There's another part of me that could use some attention."

She can't mean…

"Do you want me to rub the bump? Like a genie lamp?"

Estee goes red. "No. I, um…"
I take her hand in mine. "Tell me. It's okay."
"I want your fingers inside of me," she blurts.
Oh.
I was *not* expecting that.

54

ten

. . .

Estee

BENJI GOES STILL.

"Sex helps with preeclampsia," I hurry to add. "It's good for my health."

"You want to have sex?" he repeats slowly.

"Well, not—we don't have to have intercourse," I add quickly. "I just… your hands feel good. Like, *really* good."

He swallows. "And it won't hurt the baby?"

Quickly, I shake my head. "Not at all."

He tilts his head in thought. "So you just want—what? To ride my hand?"

"I'll take whatever you're willing to give me."

"Sex is messy," Benji says slowly.

I smirk.

"Not just physically," he continues. "Emotionally. Are you sure you're in a place where—"

"Yes," I interrupt.

"But—"

"Yes," I repeat. "I'm so goddamn horny all the fucking time. Silicone is great, but it's not doing the job anymore. I need the real thing. Please."

His jaw clenches and his hands curl into fists.

"Fine," he finally says.

"Fine?"

"Yeah. You can use me." His voice is hoarse. "How do you want to do this?"

"Well, I'd like you to not act like this is the worst thing in the world. I don't want to force you into it if you're not interested."

Benji exhales slowly. "That is not what's happening here," he says slowly.

"Then what is it?" I cross my arms over my chest and wince at my tender breasts.

His hands land on my hips. To my surprise, he lifts me effortlessly until I'm sprawled on his lap, my belly between us. I straddle his thighs, setting my hands on his shoulders.

"What is it?" I ask again.

His dark eyes are wide and warm as they rove over my body, hungry, like a caress of want and need.

That's silly. He doesn't actually *want* me. Still, it's nice to pretend. To believe in the fallacy. For a few minutes, maybe…

Benji threads his hand through my hair, gripping the back of my neck. He surges forward and captures my lips with his. I let out a muffled *oof* of surprise before he retreats.

He opens his mouth and I cover it with my hand.

"Don't say it," I plead. "It's not a mistake."

His eyes soften. His grip in my hair shifts, relaxing.

This time, when I kiss him, he isn't surprised. His lips meet mine in a cautious kiss.

But fuck, I don't want cautious. I want to be fucking railed into next week.

The first touch to my breast is careful. I cover his hand with mine, flexing my grip, and he lets out a soft pant against my lips before he deepens the kiss.

Gone is the careful, cautious roommate. He's confident as he licks into my mouth, his tongue tangling with mine. He massages the swell of my breast, and when I pull down my camisole to expose myself, he immediately moves to cover me again with his bare hand.

The friction of his calloused palm against my sensitive skin sets me on fire. I rock against his lap, desperate for another kind of friction.

Benji chuckles against my mouth as he lowers the other side of my camisole. He breaks the kiss and licks his lips. His eyes rove over my top half. The expression on his face is totally blissed out.

Really, dude? They're just boobs.

Aching and swollen boobs, maybe, but still just boobs. Just because I've gained two cup sizes doesn't mean—

He pinches at my nipple and a burst of lightning scorches through me. My pussy clenches around emptiness.

"Please," I whisper.

His fingers toy at the waistband of my sweats. As he tiptoes around my belly, I let out a grunt of frustration.

Time for playing is over. I *need* this. Need him.

Shoving his hand beneath the waistband of my sweatpants, I drag him down to my cunt. He cups me there, the steadiness of his thick fingers making me throb with want.

He threads his other hand through my hair again, gripping the back of my neck.

"Are you sure?" His voice is rough and gravelly, and I swear if he doesn't fucking touch me soon—

In answer, I kiss him again, all tongue and teeth. I'm done playing.

His finger slowly strokes the seam between my legs. I'm desperate, aching. My core is slick. Just when I think I can't stand his slow strokes any more, he slides a finger inside of me and I cry out, my head thrown back.

Clenching around him, I try to find the relief that's just out of reach.

My hands grip his shoulders as I slowly lift up and sink back down, fucking myself on his finger. A flush rises high in his cheeks and his eyes are glassy as he adds a second, twisting his wrist and scissoring his fingers.

"F—" My exhalation is cut off by his mouth slamming back onto mine.

His fingers fuck into me and he brushes his thumb across my clit with firm, steady pressure. I'm not shy as I ride his hand, taking the pleasure I so desperately need.

But it's not enough. It might never be enough.

When I break the kiss to get some breath back into my lungs, he moves his attention to my neck, kissing down the column of my throat. He continues down the swell of my breast.

When he wraps his lips around my nipple and gently bites down, I pop off like a bottle rocket. Pleasure courses through me and I clench around his fingers.

Benji stares at me with wide eyes, his pupils lust-blown. It takes me a few moments before I'm able to lift myself up and he removes his fingers from within me.

To my surprise, he brings them to his mouth, licking my taste from his fingers.

I start to throb again.

Letting out a whimper, I grab his slick hand and thread my fingers through his, kissing the back of his hand.

"Feel better?" he asks, a crooked smile on his face.

"No, actually," I snap back once I can breathe again. I shove his shoulder. "What kind of move is that?"

"What?" He looks genuinely surprised. "I thought…"

"Ugh. I just—I need—" I shift on his lap, squeezing my thighs together as best I can while straddling his.

He swallows loudly as I feel the unmistakable hardness beneath me.

I exhale slowly, my eyes lifting to his.

"I need more," I tell him honestly. "That wasn't enough to satisfy me."

He lifts me off his lap onto my feet, and before I can

protest, Benji pulls down my sweatpants and plain cotton undies. My tits are still hanging out, leaving my bump the only part of me that's covered.

Tilting his head, he studies me for a moment before he reaches for the hem of my tank top, lifting it up over my head.

I'm naked before him, but I've never felt so seen.

To my surprise, Benji lifts his hips and pulls down his gray sweatpants, revealing his hard, thick cock. The head is swollen, a dusky red, and the tip glistens with pre-cum. I want to lick it. Him. All of him.

Fuck.

"Come here," he says, reaching for my hand.

I let him pull me forward. He lifts me onto his lap, over his cock, and I settle on his thighs again. His thick length feels like heaven between my legs.

"Take what you want," Benji says. His hands settle on my waist. "Tell me what you want from me."

I swivel my hips, grinding down on his hard-on. He exhales heavily and tightens his grip on my hips.

"That's it, Es. Use me," he urges. His hips flex up, pressing himself against me. "Take what you need."

Setting a slow pace, I grind my clit along his cock to get the friction I so desperately need. His hips punch up, his pelvis rotating against mine.

"Can I touch you?" he asks.

"Please," I beg. "Please touch me."

He slides two fingers back inside me, thrusting them in and out with ruthless precision. I rut against him, fucking myself between his cock below me and his fingers inside me.

I'm so fucking close. Everything inside of me coils tight, like a spring about to burst. I've never felt like this before. Every single nerve ending is alight with pleasure, fire licking at me from inside.

When Benji slides his hand along the back of my neck and

drags my mouth back to his, I explode. Everything inside of me feels tight and loose at the same time, pliant and forgiving and yet strong and steady.

His fingers fuck me through it, not letting up until I sag against his strong chest. When he withdraws from inside of me, I let out a soft whine at the emptiness.

Benji moves his hands to my hips as his punch up, grinding his hard length along the slickness between my thighs. He rubs himself against me. I squeeze the tops of my thighs together, giving him a tight channel to fuck into.

It takes three more thrusts before he explodes with a long, loud groan. His hot cum pulses against my pussy and the lower half of my belly, some landing on his.

He lets out a heavy sigh. His hand on my upper back guides me to lean on him and I rest my face in his neck. His pulse thuds beneath my cheek, reassuring me. Of what, I'm not sure. That I'm not alone in this, maybe.

"So…" he says.

I hold my breath. "Yeah?"

Please don't say this was a mistake. Please don't—

"Anytime you need… *anything*," he says slowly. "Sign me up. I'm down."

Letting out a little giggle, I pull myself away from the warmth of his torso. "Got it. Fucking around with the pregnant chick. You're into it."

He opens his mouth to say something, then shakes his head. "Yeah. New kink unlocked," he finally says.

I climb off his lap and grab my clothes off the floor.

"Shit. I got you everywhere, didn't I?" To my surprise, he whips off his t-shirt, leaving him naked, too. He uses his shirt to wipe off my belly and between my legs.

His chest is broad and covered in a solid layer of hair, tapering down his soft belly to his spent cock.

"I'm, um…" I swallow. "I'm gonna clean up."

Benji's eyes go wide. "Did I mess up everything?"

"No. You were great," I tell him honestly. "I'm sticky and sweaty and—"

He nods slowly. "It doesn't have to be anything you don't want it to be."

I exhale heavily. "Okay. Good. So—so nothing has changed?"

He reaches for my hand, squeezing gently. I've never been more exposed.

"We're good, Estee," Benji says firmly.

eleven

. . .

Estee

I'M on cloud fucking nine. It's amazing what a couple of good orgasms will do.

When Benji invited me to his work party, I wasn't sure I wanted to go. He convinced me, though, with those soft hazel eyes and kindness etched into his face and a quiet *please*. He wants me to have fun and relax. I don't know how to tell him I haven't been relaxed since I was four years old.

Now, wearing real pants and a bra for the first time in weeks, my hair and makeup done... I'm glad I went out. It's bitterly cold, but that's okay, because I have Benji here with me to keep me warm.

When we enter the bougie bar downtown, he helps me out of my coat and folds it over his arm. I feel a little under-dressed in my dark maternity jeans and blouse, but it's too damn cold to wear any of my dresses, and I am *not* about to wear tights when I have to pee every fifteen minutes.

My roommate sets his hand on the small of my back and guides me to the back room, closed for Madison Marketing. The small space is packed full. Benji mentioned his company has about fifty employees, plus everyone who's brought a partner with them.

Not that I'm his *partner*. I'm just the roommate leeching off of his kindness. I'll pay him back. I just don't know how. Luckily, he doesn't seem to be asking—yet.

I know firsthand how quickly that can all change.

I haven't heard a peep from my ex. His empty threats about the ring were just that—empty. He may have bought the setting, but the diamond was a family heirloom, and he knows the law is on my side. He hasn't asked about the baby—but he didn't care much about the baby prior to the split, either.

With a sigh, I shake my head. Man, I sure know how to pick them.

Benji looks over at me, concern on his face. "What's wrong?"

"Nothing's wrong," I tell him automatically.

He squints at me, scrutinizing me. "Okay," he finally says. He reaches for me, setting his hand on the small of my back. "Let's go find people."

Leading me toward the throng of people, I smile and nod as we move through the crowd. He doesn't stop to chat with any of the people who give him curious looks. I don't exactly know what he does for a living. He has a graduate degree in psychology, I know, because he mentioned getting his master's at Boston College. The company is a marketing company. I'm quite intrigued.

Benji leads me to two people huddled near the buffet line. They look us over with undisguised curiosity.

"Holy fuck." The speaker is a tall blonde woman with bold brows. "You did it."

The man beside her, about the same height as her but lanky as a string bean, stares at us with wide, googly eyes.

"I think I'm hallucinating," he says.

"You two are shitheads," Benji says, shaking his head. "Guys, this is Estee. Es, Rivka and Chet, my coworkers. They *used* to be my friends," he continues with a smile. "Guess that's changed."

Rivka punches him in the shoulder. "You love us."

"You have to. It's Stockholm syndrome," Chet adds. "You're stuck with us now."

Benji squints at him. "You're not using that diagnosis correctly."

"It's a pleasure to meet you, Estee," Rivka says, offering her hand for a shake. "Call me Riv."

"Nice to meet you, Riv," I say with a genuine smile, then turn to Chet. "I think I like you guys."

Chet grins, the corner of his eyes wrinkling with delight. "Good. Because you're already one of us, so it would suck if you didn't like hanging out with us."

"Maybe now you can convince this guy to spend more time with us rather than staying late at the office or rushing home every night," Riv adds.

My eyebrows go up.

"We meet for trivia at a pub near the office on Thursdays," she continues. "Our team desperately needs more estrogen. You *have* to come join us."

Oh. So she's *not* trying to steal Benji away from me.

Not that there's anything to steal. He's a grown man and we fooled around one time. There's nothing going on. And I don't have any right to tell him not to hang out with his friends and coworkers.

"Benj mentioned you're a lawyer. That means you're smart," Chet says. "We could use more brains on our team. Right now we majorly suck at most of the categories."

"I'm not that smart," I deflect.

Benji stiffens. "Don't say that."

"I'm book smart, not trivia smart," I correct. "I know how to study and parse contracts. I'm not up to date on pop culture. That's never been what's interested me."

"What do you do for fun?" Riv asks curiously, with kindness on her face.

"I love to go hiking and being outside. These days, I'm reading a lot of romance novels." My hand rubs over my belly automatically. "Kind of difficult to go out and about right now."

Riv tilts her head. "I really admire the way you're doing this on your own. It must be really tough."

Benji squeezes my shoulder. "She's not on her own."

I draw a moment of comfort from him before I answer her. "I always knew I wanted kids, but I thought it would happen differently. I'm not going to get upset because it didn't happen the way I planned. Just putting one foot in front of the other."

My roommate frowns.

"I could use a drink," Chet announces. "Estee, can I get you anything?"

"Cranberry juice, please, if you don't mind."

"I don't." He reaches out and squeezes my arm. "Asshole, you want anything?"

"I'll go with you," Benji says.

The two of them walk away, leaving me with Riv. I'm not sure what to make of her. She gestures to a nearby table and we sit.

"So you and Benj..." she says.

My guard goes up. "Yeah?"

"He's being good to you?"

The memory of last night flashes through my mind. My cheeks heat.

"Yeah, he's great," I tell her honestly.

"I know moving in with him must have been a transition," she continues. "If you need a safe place to go, I have a spare room. In case you don't want to live with some dude."

I blink. "You don't even know me."

Riv shrugs. "He talks about you a lot. I probably shouldn't

tell you that, but I will. He talks about you all the time. And if that's something that bothers you… sometimes you just need to hear it out loud to make an informed decision."

Does it bother me? I honestly don't know.

Benji and Chet arrive with drinks. He offers me a cranberry juice—no ice, just the way I like it. There's a funny feeling in my chest. He knows I don't like ice.

He's holding a soda for himself.

"You can totally drink," I tell him. "I don't care if you have a beer or whatever."

Benji shrugs. "I don't need alcohol to have a good time."

"I'm just saying, it won't bother me if you drink."

He squeezes my shoulder with a faint smile. "Thanks. I'll keep that in mind."

We socialize with some of his coworkers. Their names go in one ear and out the other. When a few people express surprise at Benji having a pregnant date, he smiles enigmatically and moves the conversation along.

Chet and Riv are great. It's easy to see why they get along so well. He's a goofy, overgrown man-child with a heart of gold. She's sarcastic and sly. Together, they balance each other out.

I like to think that together, Benji and I balance each other out, too. He cares for me, always looking for a way to make me feel safe and protected. And when I'm with him, I do. I know he'll let no harm come to me—or my baby.

After a few hours of socializing, I'm starting to flag. Benji has started saying goodbye to some of his coworkers and it couldn't come a moment too soon. Chet pulls me into a hug and so Riv does, too.

"We'll have to grab coffee sometime," she says, and I wholeheartedly believe her offer is genuine. "I know how it can be when you're new to town. We'll arrange something."

Benji has a pleased smile on his face, and as he looks between us, his eyes soften. "Thanks, Riv," he says warmly.

He wraps his arm around my shoulders as he steers me away. After grabbing our coats, he helps me into mine, then sets his arm around me as we wait for the rideshare.

"Did you have a good time?" he asks curiously.

"I did, yeah. Thanks for bringing me." It was nice to get out of the apartment for a bit, spend some time with other adult humans.

"Estee, it was entirely my pleasure."

His voice is rich and gravelly, and my heart starts to flutter double-time.

Benji swallows, his eyes on mine. He seems to make a decision because he ducks his head.

The shrill sound of a car honk cuts through the air, the driver of our rideshare apparently not in a waiting mood.

Benji shakes his head, reaching for my hand. "Come on," he mutters. "Let's go home."

twelve

. . .

Benji

"I THINK I MESSED UP," I blurt.

Asher cuts off his conversation about his wedding. "What did you do?"

We're in the middle of a crowded street in downtown Cambridge. We're supposed to be meeting up with Yoni and Elliott for lunch.

My face flushes. "Um…"

"Did you and Estee finally hook up?" my best friend asks.

I stop in my tracks. "What?" *She told him?*

To my surprise, Asher laughs. "Come on, dude. You've had a thing for her forever."

My guard up, I nod. "I wasn't aware that was common knowledge."

"Well, when you come to stay at my house for a week in high school and we spend the entire time with you following the girls around and making cow eyes at Estee, I'd say it's fairly obvious," he says dryly.

"I did not make *cow eyes* at her," I mutter, bundling into my coat.

He laughs. "Okay, dude. Whatever."

"Why'd you bring her to me, then? Yoni and El have a spare room."

Asher raises his eyebrows. "Are you upset to have a roommate? Or are you upset because it's her?"

"I'm not *upset*," I explain delicately. "I thought you'd care more about her than dropping her off with someone who may or may not have had a thing for her once upon a time very long ago."

He laughs outright. "Sure, bud."

"Ash…"

He seems to realize I'm not playing, because he turns to me in the middle of the street. "Look, I trust you, and I know you want the best for her. She's safe with you. That's what matters to me."

"So you weren't trying to matchmake?"

He shrugs, making an *eh* movement with his hand. "I wouldn't be upset if something were to happen."

"But…"

"Look, I've known you almost twenty years. Estee is the sister I never had. If there's anyone I trust to treat her right, it's you."

"I will," I tell him seriously. I don't take his trust lightly.

"So…" He waggles his eyebrows. "Did you two finally hook up?"

"We… messed around," I hedge.

Ash holds up his hand for a high five. "Nice."

"You're seriously okay hearing about this? If some guy were to talk about my sister…"

He shrugs. "Sex helps lower the risk of pre-eclampsia, which I know she's worried about. It's healthy for her. And for you, you goddamn monk. Getting off regularly will lower your risk of prostate cancer."

"Technically—" I cut off. He doesn't need to know that we didn't have full penetrative intercourse. We exchanged mutual orgasms. That counts as sex in my book.

Besides, preeclampsia is for pregnant people with high blood pressure, and on top of that, the research is iffy on whether sex will actually help prevent it. If it makes her feel better, though, I'm happy to volunteer.

We're stopped in front of a boutique, and as people push around us, I look at the storefront for the first time.

It's a baby boutique. It's full of baby stuff.

"Let's go in," I tell Asher.

He frowns. "We'll be late."

"It'll be worth it," I promise.

Inside, we're assaulted by the scent of baby powder. There's a few pieces of furniture around, but mostly what captures my attention is the clothes.

So. Many. Baby. Clothes.

"How many outfits does a kid need, anyway?" Asher mutters under his breath.

I half agree with him as I look around.

And when I spot a little onesie with green dinosaurs... My heart twists, thinking of how Estee's baby will look in it. I don't know the gender or even what the baby will look like, but I know that the baby will be adorable in this.

"I'm getting this," I announce.

Asher raises his eyebrows. "You are?"

"The baby needs it." I nod solemnly.

Laughing, he picks up a basket and throws the outfit in. "Okay. So what else does the baby need?"

We traipse through the store, and nine times out of ten, when I imagine the baby in the little lion pajama set or the little sweatsuit with frogs on it, I know the baby needs it.

Estee needs it.

"I don't know what we're going to do about the big stuff," I admit to Asher as we shop. "We don't have a car. Do I have to get a car for her to have a car seat?"

"Hold up," he says. "Why would *you* get a car for *her* to use the car seat?"

I shrug. "I don't know."

He shakes his head. "Fuck, you are so far gone for her."

"Yeah." I don't even try to deny it. "But she doesn't—"

Asher rolls his eyes. "Just talk to her."

I chew my lip.

"Look, if you guys are fucking around, she deserves to know how you feel," he points out. "It's not fair to her if you hide it."

"She doesn't feel the same way."

He squints at me. "So you're not using the baby as an excuse anymore?"

"I don't want her to write me off as a fun time. If she lets me, I'll be here for her through this."

"And beyond?" He frowns. "It's not going to change things when she pops out the baby? You aren't going to want her to move out?"

Waving a hand at the baby store around us, I stare at him point blank. "I'm not running away. I'm doing the *opposite* of it, actually. And it fucking scares me shitless, knowing she doesn't feel the same."

"Benj—"

"I'm fun for now, but she doesn't want a future with me. She doesn't want *me*." My breaths are coming faster now, my heart racing. I try to swallow the panic rising within me. It doesn't want to dissipate. It wants to settle in and cling to my internal organs.

Asher steps toward me, setting his hand on my shoulder and squeezing. "And has she said that with words? Or are you jumping to conclusions?"

I open my mouth.

"Have you two had an open, honest conversation about where you want to go?"

Exhaling slowly, I hang my head. "No."

"Well, that might be a good place to start."

I have the distinct impression he's laughing at me.

"Fuck off," I mutter, shoving his hand away.

Asher laughs in earnest now. "Come on. Let's buy some cute baby clothes, then let's grab lunch and get day-drunk."

We spend another twenty minutes in the store. More little outfits end up in my basket than not. I stay away from frilly pink things, knowing Estee wants the baby to have gender neutral options.

"What about this one?" I ask, holding up a set of dinosaur footie pajamas with claws on the feetsies.

Asher makes a face. "I don't know, man."

"Come on. Dinosaurs are totally gender neutral."

"No, I agree with that," he says mildly. "But don't you already have, like, four different dinosaur outfits?"

I sag. "Yeah. I guess so."

He sighs. "Five can't hurt, then."

Perking up as I toss the outfit into my overflowing basket, I finally allow him to convince me it's time to check out. And as I fork over the better part of a paycheck in cute little baby clothes, all I can think about is Estee holding our baby in one of these outfits.

Hold up.

Our baby? When did the baby become *mine*?

I mean… I'm allowing Estee to live in my house. And I'd love for us to get together, to really try to make something of ourselves.

The baby, though…

A heaviness lifts from my chest. I want this baby. I didn't expect to have a kid at this stage of my life, but if there's one thing I know for certain, it's that I want to help Estee raise this baby.

I just need to convince her first.

thirteen

· · ·

Estee

WHEN BENJI WALKED in the door after his lunch with Asher, he was so drunk, he stumbled into the doorway and nearly took out the entryway console table. I don't think he even saw me working in the kitchen. He walked into the apartment, dropped shopping bags on the floor, and collapsed face-first into his bed. His soft snores echoed around the empty apartment, in concert with the 90s pop playlist I had going.

I didn't expect him to drink so much. Is this to make up for not drinking last night?

I've finished work and cleared away my things by the time he emerges from his room, looking adorably rumpled. He's changed into an old Penn State t-shirt and gray sweatpants.

"Hey," he says, padding into the kitchen. He drops a kiss to the top of my head and continues to the fridge, pulling out glass containers with leftovers.

I freeze. "What was that?"

He blinks slowly at me. "What was what?"

"You—you just kissed me."

He chokes. "I did?"

"Did you not realize?"

Benji's face flushes. "No?"

"O…kay." Sidestepping that, I ask, "How was lunch?"

"It was good. Nice to catch up with Yoni and El." He pauses. "I, um, I got you something."

"You didn't have to get me anything," I say automatically.

He shakes his head. "Let's light the candles first."

Pulling out the menorah, I let him set up the candles and he hands me the matches. As I light the first candle, he takes my hand, and together we say the blessings.

After, he disappears into his room, coming back with the enormous bags I saw him with earlier.

"These are for you," he says, thrusting the bags toward me.

"Benji—I can't—"

"Take it." He ducks his head, a shy smile on his face. "I want you to have it."

Slowly, I reach into the first bag, pulling out a onesie.

I gape at him. "You bought me baby clothes?"

His face flushes. "Yeah. I saw it and—I just, you needed it."

Pulling out another little outfit, I look at the tiny clothes, then back at him.

"You did this? For me?"

He shrugs. "I'm growing attached to the little one. They're not even here yet and I already think they're a pretty cool person."

My heart squeezes. "You do?"

"Yeah. You're their mom," he says, like it's that simple. "That automatically makes them cool."

Mom.

I'm going to be someone's mom.

Tears spring to my eyes as my hand moves to my belly. I haven't let myself think much about what happens after the baby's born. There's so much up in the air. Hell, the baby might not even arrive on the date I'm expecting them. The point of a due date is that it's an estimation, and that drives me nuts. And then there's the whole labor thing… Who knows how long that will take?

The baby kicks, right where my hand is.

My eyes dart up to Benji's. I feel the need to say something… but I'm not sure what. Just that something needs to be said.

He opens his mouth.

And somehow, I just know that what he wants to say… it won't be good. It's not going to be what I want to hear.

"Tea! I need tea!" The words jumble out of my mouth.

Benji blinks twice, then a slow smile spreads over his face. He ambles to his feet and grabs the kettle. "What kind of tea do you want?"

"You don't have to—"

"I want to," he says, like it's that simple. He looks over his shoulder at me. "Don't read into it, Estee. I wanted to."

As the water boils, he heats up two plates with leftovers. There are days where I can stomach real food and days where I can only tolerate yogurt and applesauce. I've been able to keep everything down for a continuous seventy-two hours, which is almost a record for me.

"Do you want to watch a movie?" he asks as he sets a plate down in front of me, taking the stool beside mine.

"Sure. What did you have in mind?"

He flushes and ducks his head, and it makes me smile.

"What is it?"

"I kind of want to watch *Eight Crazy Nights*," he admits.

"The Adam Sandler cartoon?"

Benji nods. "Yeah. I know it's a kids' cartoon, but—"

"But it's a great movie," I interrupt. "I can't decide which is better, the Rugrats Chanukah or Passover episodes."

"Passover. Hands down."

Smiling, I arch an eyebrow. "How are you so sure?"

"Because it's better," he says, like that answers it. "I probably haven't watched them since college." He pauses, then adds, "I was a chapter advisor for the youth group all through school. We watched them every year."

"So you like working with kids?"

I don't know why that sends a warm, fluttery feeling through me. The baby kicks again, and I move my hand to my lower belly.

"I like kids, yeah." Benji gives me a self-deprecating smile. "I wanted to go into children's psychology."

"And instead you ended up in advertising?"

He shrugs. "I couldn't deal with seeing so many young, traumatized kids day in and day out. So instead I work on the psychological messaging in children's advertising, trying to bring some levity to their lives."

Huh. "I didn't know that's what you did."

"I mean, I also work on ads for adults. And we're definitely trying to sell our products," he adds. "I'm not a superhero by any means. It's a job. I'd rather it be done by someone who has their best interests in mind."

"You do," I say quietly. Because I know he cares. It's evident in everything he does, how much he cares.

If he can go out of his way to cook for me, to draw me a bath, to bring me presents just because, to curl up on the couch beside me, to help me get off when I so desperately need it...

My breath catches.

I can repay him.

I don't know that it'll be enough. It might never be enough to show how much I appreciate him and all he's done for me over the last few weeks.

Leaning over, I set my hand on his thigh. His muscles tense beneath my touch.

His eyes dart to mine. His tongue comes out to wet his lips. He turns on his stool to face me, my hand still on his leg.

"Wh-what are you doing?" His voice comes out as a croak.

"I want to do something for you," I tell him slowly.

"Okay…" He watches me expectantly.

I bet he's thinking I'll say something like he should take a bubble bath or go take a nap.

Taking a deep breath, I meet his eyes.

"I want to suck your dick."

Benji stops breathing.

And just when I think he's about to run out of air, he lets out a gusty sigh and reaches for me. He pulls me off my stool and into the space between his legs, bracketing me in.

His lips come crashing down onto mine, his hand diving into my hair to hold me close. Our tongues tangle and dance as he sips kisses from my lips.

My hands fist in his t-shirt, pulling him closer, or me, or both. All I know is there is entirely too much space between us. I want to be flush together, no separation from my breath to his, from my heart beating to his.

Benji wrenches himself away, gasping for breath. His lips are slick and swollen from my kisses.

"We can't," he says.

"Why not?" I ask.

"We—I—"

I cock my head. "Is the reason because you don't want to? Or because you feel like you should say no?"

"The second one." His pupils are dilated, his eyes wide and unblinking. "You—I—*ungh.*"

I try to extract myself from his grasp, but his hand is solid on my hip, his thighs keeping me steady.

"Why do you feel like you should say no?" I gaze at him with what I hope is a non-judgmental expression. He liked when we fooled around the other night. I'd think he'd be down for it again.

Benji lets out a strangled sound from deep in his throat. "Because you don't mean it."

I squeeze his thigh again. "What makes you think I don't intend to follow through?"

He shakes his head, unable to answer me.

"Is it because I'm pregnant? Do I turn you off?"

"No," he says forcefully, and I blink at how serious he is. "Estee, that's not it, at all."

"What, so because I'm pregnant—"

"It's fucking hot," Benji blurts.

It's my turn to pause.

"Seeing you like this, bringing new life into the world... I want you, I don't want you to doubt that." His eyes bore into mine. "I just don't think this is a good idea."

Oh.

Okay.

My eyes well up with unshed tears, and I turn my head away.

But he still won't release me.

His big hand comes up to my cheek, tilting my head back until I meet his eyes again.

"I don't want to upset you," he says.

"You didn't," I lie.

"Things are getting messy," Benji says slowly. "Trust me when I say that I'm trying to protect you when—"

"I don't need you to *protect* me," I snap. "I'm a big girl. I can handle myself."

He swallows loudly.

"What? Got something else to say?" I demand.

"I'm trying to protect myself, too," he says quietly.

My head snaps back, as if I've been slapped. "From what? From me?"

"From everything," he says.

"I thought you wanted to fuck around with the pregnant chick."

His eyes flash. "Don't. Don't belittle yourself like that."

"Dude, I'm offering you no-strings-attached sex, and you're just, what, walking away?"

"I can't do no strings attached," he finally says. "It's getting complicated."

"So, what, you don't want to do this? That's not what you said two nights ago when I—"

"I know." He releases me and runs a hand through his hair. "I *know*. I thought I could do this. I could handle it. But…"

I take a step back. "But you're not interested."

"I'm interested." Benji meets my eyes. "It's not a matter of interest. It's just not a good idea."

"Right. Okay." I cross my arms over my chest. "Maybe I should look into moving out, then."

"No." I'm surprised by his vehemence. "I don't want you to move out. I'll get over it, over this. Just… don't leave."

Don't leave me.

That's what I *want* him to say.

But we're not together. We aren't a couple. We're just two people who live in the same apartment. Until I moved in, I hadn't seen him in more than a decade. I wouldn't have even classified him as a friend.

And now…

"I need some space," I tell him, and he swallows, nodding.

"If that's what you think is best."

Making my way to my bedroom, I crawl into the bed and pull the covers up over my face. Nobody wants me. They say they do, but they don't actually want me around. Sometimes I wonder why I even try anymore.

Silently, I cry myself to sleep.

fourteen

. . .

Benji

STUPID ASHER and his stupid Chanukah party. I don't want to be here. I don't want to be home, either.

Annoyed, I nurse my beer and watch as my friends have a good time around me. *They* aren't excessively pissed off. *They* don't have epically foul moods tonight. *They* aren't majorly avoiding going home to their pregnant roommate they've been stewing over the last two days.

Yeah. So there's that.

Estee has been keeping her distance and I've been doing my best to give her space. As soon as I get home from work, she disappears into her bedroom, and I've been hiding out in mine, too, so she can have the main room to herself if she wants it.

Chet and Riv have been giving me extra breathing room at work, too. He brought me coffee and a donut, then sat in his chair and didn't talk to me for almost three hours, which is basically forever. Riv asked once how Estee is doing, and whatever she saw on my face made her turn around to her desk and leave me alone.

I don't know what I want. I know I want Estee, something semi-permanent and not at all casual. But I don't know where to go beyond that. Do we date? Do we rush into something more?

It would help if I knew where she stood, but all she's offered me is sex. Maybe that's a sign I should drop it. I can't do something physical without their being an emotional connection, and if she can't handle the emotions…

My eyes flit across the room to where she's charming Elliott and Yoni with some story requiring excessive hand motions. My annoyance dials up a notch at the adoring look on Yoni's face. He loves her.

Why wouldn't he? She's awesome.

Turning on my heel, I make my way to the spare bedroom. It's blessedly empty. Throwing myself onto the bed, I cover my face with my hands.

I thought I could do this. I should have known.

At the same time, though, I don't want her to move out. That means it's over. That means there's no chance of anything happening. It's not like she's going to move in with me, move somewhere else, and then move back in—and with a baby, no less.

No. I have to keep her with me. I have to prove to her that staying with me is a good idea—for both her and the baby.

I just have to figure out a way to get over my shit first.

The door creaks open, and I silently groan at my hiding space being found out. Instead, I'm pleasantly surprised when the subtle scent of gardenias fills the air.

Estee.

The bed dips down and she crawls up beside me.

I crack open an eye.

"Can I lay here with you?" she asks.

I nod.

"I've missed you." Her words are quiet.

"I was giving you space."

She sighs. "I know. I can miss you and need space at the same time."

Sinking onto the bed, she rolls onto her side facing away from me.

And then she reaches back behind her, grabbing my arm and wrapping it around her. I curl into her body, spooning her from behind.

"That's better," she says with a happy-sounding sigh.

Tentatively, I let my hand fall to her belly, and while she tenses for a second, she lets out a soft noise and relaxes into me. I run my hand over the lower part of her abdomen, soothing little strokes.

"Nobody's done this," she says.

"Done what?"

"Touched my bump."

I pull my hand away.

And then she's reaching for me again, setting my hand back on her swollen belly.

"I like it," Estee says quietly. "It's a part of me. I'm so fucking starved for physical contact."

My blood runs cold. Is that all I am to her? A means to an end?

"I've missed the little touches," she says, still facing away from me. "I liked when you kissed me the other day."

I can kiss her all the fucking time if she'd like.

Somehow, I know she's not talking about the charged kiss we had after dinner. She's referring to the way I kissed her head as I passed through the kitchen.

I wasn't intending to do it. It was a reflex.

But that doesn't mean it wasn't real.

When I'm in a relationship, I'm an affectionate guy. I like to hold my partner's hand in public, hug and hold them when we're relaxing on the couch, and curl up beside them in bed. Innocent displays of affection—a kiss on the cheek or on the temple, a squeeze of an arm or a shoulder, a hand on their leg when we're in the car.

I get affection from my friends, but it's not the same as the touch of a partner. Asher is always ready for a bear hug. Elliott prefers to show their love through food. Chet, too. Yoni is a caretaker, always collecting houseplants.

"I really liked the other night," Estee continues. "When we…" She clears her throat.

"When we had sex?" I ask mildly.

She turns to look at me over her shoulder. "We didn't—it was—"

"A mutual exchange of orgasms. That's sex to me."

Humming under her breath, she settles again, her head on the pillow beside mine. "But we can't do it again."

"It's not a good idea," I repeat.

I want to. Fuck knows, I want to. But that doesn't mean we *should*.

"I'm not good at keeping things casual. And you mean too much to me to jeopardize our friendship," I explain. My hand roves over her belly. "This little one deserves to have a stable living situation. And so do you."

She inhales sharply. "So self-sacrificing."

I can't tell if she's being sarcastic or not.

"I like having you at home with me. It's nice. Helps the apartment not feel so lonely."

"Bet you won't say that when the newborn is crying all through the night," she mutters.

Holding her close, I nuzzle my nose into the back of her hair.

"I will. And I'll keep saying it, until you believe me. *Because it's true.*"

I can't let myself think too much about what happens after the baby is born. I'd like for Estee and myself to be adults about it, but my juvenile side wants to take claim over her as mine. Over both of them.

If Estee wanted a father for her baby, I'd step in and help her raise them as my own. If she wanted a husband for herself, I want to be the first guy she calls.

That's the exact opposite of casual. And I can't keep pretending what I want doesn't matter. I can't convince her to let me in, but I can protect my heart from getting trampled even further.

Estee's soft breaths slow, and I peek an eye over at her slack face. She's snoozing, her eyes fluttering as she dreams.

Snuggling in closer, I hold her tight and let myself indulge in the moment. When she wakes up, I'm sure she'll put more distance between us. Get things back to normal.

Until then, I'm going to hold the woman I've had a thing for since I learned how to want, and pretend like she wants me, too.

fifteen

. . .

Estee

THE DOORBELL RINGS, and I turn to look at the
offending noise like it's going to answer me.

Heaving myself to my feet, I pad slowly to the door, ready
to tell the salesman to go away.

But it's not a salesman. It's Arielle.

"You suck," she says when the door swings open.

"Excuse me?" My eyebrows arch up.

"You disappeared on me," she accuses. "You came to the
party last night and then hid away all night."

With a sigh, I nod and step back to let her in. "I did. I'm
sorry."

"I miss you, boo." She gives me a tight hug, and knowing
her sensory issues, I hold her back tightly with firm pressure.
"I'm worried about you."

"I'm worried about me, too," I admit.

Immediately, I head to the kitchen to put the kettle on, and
she settles on a barstool at the counter. Grabbing two mugs, I
fill them with hot cocoa powder.

"Do you want to talk about it?"

"Kind of want to avoid it," I tell her.

She laughs. "Yeah, that sounds like you." She pauses. "You're not heading for another depressive episode?"

"Nah. I'm still taking meds, and my doctor's set me up with a psychiatrist. I see them in early January."

"And the baby's due…" Arielle's eyebrows go up.

"End of January."

She laughs. "Cutting it kind of close, Es."

"Yeah, well, doctors suck." The kettle whistles and I pour her hot chocolate, then mine. "Just establishing myself as a new patient in a new city was almost impossible."

"But you did?" She looks at me pointedly.

"Yeah. I have an appointment tomorrow." I blow on my cocoa to cool it before I take a sip. "Everything has been looking good so far, but I know they were concerned about my weight, so…"

"You are all baby." Arielle shakes her head. "It's like everything you've gained is in your belly."

"That's kind of the goal."

I know what she's talking about. I was borderline underweight when I got pregnant, thanks to a rough couple years after law school. And then getting sick nearly every day, multiple times a day… I get why she's concerned, though, especially with my disordered eating background.

I'm in a healthy mental place, though. I'm not triggered by it, I'm doing fairly well, and I don't have obsessive thoughts. That has to be a good thing.

She looks at me carefully. "Are you okay?"

I shake my head. "I'm fine."

Arielle laughs. "That's your favorite word these days. You're always fine."

"I *am*," I insist. "You don't have to worry about me. I can take care of myself."

"Don't you get it?" She takes my hand. "Babe, I'm always going to worry about you. That's my job."

I swallow. "But—"

"We're family. We've been friends since we were six years old," she continues. "The guy I'm marrying is basically your brother. Like it or not—and I hope you like it—we're stuck with each other."

There's a lump in my throat. "I like it," I tell her quietly.

"Good." Arielle squeezes my hand. "I do, too."

We drink our cocoa quietly.

"Come on," she says. "Let's go for a walk. I could use some retail therapy. Have you organized your registry yet?"

I shake my head. "I have a lot of baby clothes." My eyes well up. Benji went out of his way to get me gender neutral outfits in the animal theme I'd mentioned.

"Well, let's get you some other things you'll need."

"I can't afford—"

"I'm not saying we'll buy everything," Arielle continues. "My mom says she wants to get you some gifts, though, and I know Asher's mom was talking about a car seat. So let's make a registry. That way, when they buy gifts, it's the stuff you actually want rather than the stuff they think you want."

I hem and haw. "I don't know…"

"I know the halacha is against it," she says. "We're not trying to summon the dark spirit. We're being prepared for someone unrelated to you wanting to buy you a present."

Jewish law, or halacha, is expressly against baby showers. We won't even say *congratulations* upon announcement of a pregnancy—not until the baby is born. There are other phrases we use to express joy at someone becoming pregnant, ways we can ward off the negative forces in the universe. We don't want to risk anything negative happening to someone experiencing joy.

It's mysticism and superstition, and I'm not sure how much I believe in it, but it's what I know. And what I know is that you don't host baby showers. Bridal showers, either.

Registries, though…

"It's practical," Arielle pushes.

With a sigh, I give in. "Let me get my coat."

She gives a little cheer.

Together, we head out and across town to the baby megastore. When I tell the shop clerk I have no idea what I'm doing, they give me a laser gun and a packet of SKUs.

"See what you like," Arielle says. "We don't expect everything to be purchased. We just want to make sure it's what you want and not all pink or all blue anything."

Laughing, I give in. "Okay. Let's do this."

Over the course of two and a half hours, we go through the entire store, scanning items we think I might need or want. I've already done research into car seats and strollers, so I have an idea of what I'd like.

The rest of it? I didn't know babies needed that much *stuff*.

None of my friends have had babies yet. If it hadn't happened the way it did, I wouldn't have planned it for myself this way, either.

But now? I wouldn't change one thing.

Things are not going according to plan. But maybe my plan needed to be thrown out. Maybe it was time for something new.

I'm getting a new start. I can be anyone that I want to be. How many people get a fresh slate?

Woah. I'm getting a little woozy.

Clutching at my belly, I lower myself into a nearby rocking chair. It's not something I particularly find comfortable, but it's better than collapsing on the floor again.

Arielle, realizing I've fallen behind her, hurries to my side. "Are you okay?"

"Just need a moment."

"Have the episodes been getting better?"

I shrug. "Some days are better than others. We've been walking a lot today."

She frowns. "Do you want me to get you a wheelchair?"

"No. I'm good. I just need a minute." Breathing carefully, I try to restore my equilibrium. I've had issues with my blood pressure from the beginning. It's how I found out I was pregnant; I had a low blood pressure episode and fainted, and the ER doc told me I was knocked up. Given that we hadn't been trying, it was a surprise.

But not insurmountable.

It's too early for me to be *excited* about the baby. Too much of my mental energy is wrapped up in *what ifs*. They're just barely viable right now. I need to keep them inside of me for a little while longer.

When Benji brought home the baby clothes, though... I started to think about dressing my baby in them, holding them in my arms and playing with them, loving them unconditionally. It felt more concrete than a scan on an ultrasound.

Because I haven't met them yet, but I already know them. I am going to love this baby so fucking much. I've already started.

And now... I blow out a breath. Now I have to get ready for them.

Lifting the baby store's scanner, I hold it up like James Bond, and I'm rewarded when Arielle grins at me.

"Let's do this."

sixteen

. . .

Estee

ARIELLE DROPS me off at home after a nice, long girls'
day. It was good to spend the time with her. I hadn't realized
how much I missed the normalcy of our friendship.

The front room of the apartment is conspicuously clean.
Like, even more clean than it should be.

Did Benji have a cleaning person come in while I was out?

As I hang up my coat, he comes out of my room, looking
guilty. Oh shit. Did I leave my dildo out?

Wait.

Why was he in my room??

"Hey," he says, his face pink. "I didn't know you were
home."

"I just got here." My eyes narrow. "Do you need
something?"

"Yeah. You."

He darts forward and takes my hand, pulling me toward
my bedroom.

"I thought you said you didn't want to have sex again."

"That's not—no." Benji shakes his head. "Just come here."

He opens the door and my heart starts to flutter.

Because there, beside my bed, is a crib.

"You did this?" My eyes well with tears.

He did this—for me. He went out of his way to build a fucking *crib*.

He nods. "Yeah. Arielle let me know the coast was clear."

"I'm going to kill her," I laugh.

"Let's avoid murder, please," he says with a shy smile. "Do… do you like it?"

I look at him, and I finally *see* him for the first time. He's good-looking, I've noticed before. But it's never really registered just how beautiful he is.

His dark hair, his hazel eyes. The five o'clock shadow on his strong jaw. He's taller than me, but not so tall that I have to jump to kiss him.

Because I want to.

No, I *need* to.

Launching myself across the room, I hurl myself into his arms, and he catches me effortlessly. My mouth crashes into his, telling him all the things I can't verbalize.

I've never had a friend who does the things he does for me. Even though I'm sure he'd chalk it up to the gift-giving season, he's gone out of his way to shower me with gifts. He could have stopped at one. Or even two. *And* they're for me as much as they're for the baby. He sees *me*, not just the bump. I'm more than an incubator to him.

The last few months, I've felt lost. First I was alone in a relationship, then I was alone and single. Once I moved to Boston, I was never *lonely*, not with Benji around. He's made sure I know I have a safe place to rest my head and a safe space to share my thoughts.

Not that I have. Not with anyone. I've kept it bottled up inside of me, afraid to let it out.

And to my surprise, as he kisses me back, some of that burden dissipates.

I'm not alone.

I don't know what this thing between us is. I don't know

what will happen. All I know is, I like him, and I liked fucking around with him, and I want to do it again. And again.

But he doesn't want that, or so he says. The way he's kissing me back tells me there's more left unsaid.

Benji walks me forward until the back of my legs hit the edge of my bed. Breaking the kiss, he maneuvers me until I'm sitting on the edge of the bed.

And then he sinks to his knees.

"Wh-what are you doing?" I run my hand through his short curls.

"I want to make you feel good." He says it like it's that easy.

"I thought you didn't want to fool around."

His eyes flutter closed and he inhales sharply. "I don't."

I'm confused.

"But—"

"I don't know what I want," he says, and I think that might be the honest truth. "All I know is right now, I'm going to go crazy if I don't get to taste you." He ducks his head, then looks up at me. "Can I?"

A bolt of lust strikes through me. I swallow as all my blood rushes south. There's a slickness now between my legs, and I try to affect a calm, collected expression.

"Go ahead. Get on with it."

His grin is positively devious as his hands move to the waistband of my leggings. I lift up to help as he pulls them down and off my legs, tossing them somewhere behind him.

I expect him to go for my underwear next.

Instead, he buries his face in my pussy and inhales deeply. My cheeks heat. He lets out a satisfied sound and then reaches for the waistband of my panties. He flings them away.

Benji pauses, staring at my exposed cunt. I'm practically vibrating with unbridled need.

"Is this what you wanted?" I can't hide the nerves in my voice.

He spreads my legs farther, eyes glued to my core. And then when his eyes dart up to mine, I see my own nerves reflected in his.

"You don't have to do anything you don't want to do," I tell him gently. I can find a vibrator and take care of myself. I can…

He swallows, his Adam's apple bobbing in his throat, and I find myself momentarily mesmerized by the simple, human reaction.

His hands slide under my ass, pulling me closer to the edge of the bed. And then he lowers his mouth to my pussy and *licks*. His tongue slides through my folds, delving inside my pussy, and then he moves to suck on the engorged bundle of nerves.

I let myself fall back against the bed and enjoy the ride. The sharp prickles of his late evening stubble scrape against the sensitive skin on my inner thighs, grounding me.

Pleasure ripples through me. I haven't been touched in *so fucking long*, and it's been even longer since I've been able to approach sex as anything other than a chore or a bargaining chip. I want to enjoy it for what it is: fun.

Benji devours me like a man facing his last meal. He strokes my thighs and runs his hands over my legs before his fingers return to my core, stroking through my folds and then pausing at my entrance.

When I tilt my hips, he slides two fingers inside of me, and the sudden fullness makes me gasp.

He pulls back immediately. "Are you okay?"

Hurriedly, I nod. "Do that again."

His eyes locked on mine, he withdraws and thrusts his fingers back into me. My eyes nearly roll back inside my head.

"Ungh."

Lips curving into a satisfied smirk, he lowers his mouth to me and continues his ministrations. I let myself fall back and indulge in the pleasure he's giving me. Willingly. He wants this as much as I do.

And as he presses on that fleshy spot on my front wall, I give in and let the pieces fall where they may. Pleasure courses through me, rolling waves of *need* and *want* and *more*.

When I finally stop trembling, Benji sits back on his heels and pulls his fingers from within me, then brings them to his lips and sucks them clean.

I let out a whimper.

"You okay?" His voice is gravelly and thick.

"Mm. Come here." Propping myself up on one elbow, I motion weakly for him.

With a chuckle, he stands and leans over me. "Hi."

Yanking him by the collar of his t-shirt, I pull him to me and kiss him thoroughly. He tastes like me. I like it.

I need more. Even though I just came, I need more. I need *him*.

Benji sets his hands on either side of my hips. He's so careful not to touch me. Sometimes he treats me like I'm so fucking fragile.

Breaking the kiss, I pull at the hem of his t-shirt. "Take this off," I demand.

He arches an eyebrow. "Excuse me?"

"Your pants, too." I reach for the waistband of his sweats.

"Estee, what..." He swallows. "What are you asking of me?"

"I want you to fuck me."

When he brings a hand to cup my cheek, I almost think he's going to say no. That it's too messy. We're friends and, for now, we're roommates. That's all we are.

Instead, he kisses me, soft and slow. When he pulls back, he whips off his shirt and then drops his sweats and boxer-briefs. His cock slaps up to rest against his soft belly.

As I scramble back against the pillows, I realize I'm still wearing my top, but when I go to take it off, he's there to help.

He lets out a guttural groan at the sight of my bra. It's a boring black sports bra with a clasp in the front. It's nothing to get excited about. They're just boobs.

When he buries his face in my swollen breasts, I have to wonder if I underestimated myself.

He kisses up my chest and up the column of my neck. When I shiver, he nuzzles the spot beneath my jaw, and I waste no time in grabbing for him, pulling him close.

"I don't want to hurt you," he murmurs.

"You won't."

Wrapping my legs around his waist, I bring us in direct, intimate contact. The feeling of his hard length pressed against my core makes me dizzy.

"Please," I tell him. "Please fuck me."

He pulls back, a frown on his face. "I don't have any condoms."

I tilt my head. "Do we need one?"

"I mean…"

"I can't get any *more* pregnant," I point out. "Have you been tested recently?"

He nods. "I'm good there. I just… I've never gone without a condom before."

Swallowing, I force myself to back up. "If you don't want to, if that's a hard boundary for you, we don't have to. I can use a toy or—"

"You're sure you're okay with it?" he asks.

"I just want you inside of me."

Benji closes his eyes, muttering curses under his breath.

And then to my surprise, he grabs two pillows, sliding them under my hips. I spread my legs and his eyes zero in on my cunt, his pupils blown.

"Fuck, Estee," he says, shaking his head.

I cock my head, watching him.

"You have no idea how long I've wanted this." His eyes snap to mine. "You're gorgeous."

Grabbing for him, I bring him close for a kiss, all tongues and teeth.

He notches his cock at my entrance, and when I exhale, he slowly thrusts inside. His muscles tense and the cords in his neck stand out in stark relief.

"Holy fuck," he breathes.

He buries himself to the hilt and goes still. I can feel my core throb around his thick length inside of me, adjusting to his size.

I expect him to get to it, to start pounding away. But Benji drops closer, his hands propping him up so he doesn't crush the bump, and he kisses me. It's gentle and sweet.

Threading my hand through his curls, I grip his hair tightly in my fist. I tilt my hips and grind my pelvis against his.

He chuckles against my lips before pulling back. He spreads my legs farther, as far as they can go, his palms keeping them open. With a few short, shallow thrusts, his motions sends sparks zipping up my spine. My eyes drift closed and I have to work to keep them open. I want to watch the pleasure crossing his face and brightening his eyes.

His brow is creased as he concentrates, swiveling his hips until he finds that spot that makes me gasp and clench around him. Benji lets out a soft groan as his cock pistons in and out of me, relentless.

Everything inside of me feels coiled tight, like a spring about to explode. My core throbs around the thick length inside of me. And when I tip over the edge, my belly contracts, and I gasp out loud. My hands fly to my bump.

Benji stops immediately, pulling out. "What's wrong?"

"I'm fine," I'm quick to assure him.

He presses a quick kiss to my lips, then rolls over beside me. His cock is pointing up, slick from being inside of me.

"I don't want to hurt you," he says softly.

"You won't." My face heats. "Sometimes when I come I get a contraction. But I'm not in labor. It's too soon."

"Yeah, no, that doesn't make me feel better," Benji says.

"Can I…" I swallow. "Can I make you feel better?"

My hand moves to his chest, then down until I reach his cock. It's thick, slick, and as I squeeze my fist around his length, he lets out a shuddery breath.

"We don't have to do anything you don't want to do," he says.

"Shut up and kiss me," I tell him.

With a laugh, he pulls me into his arms and kisses me. I stroke him, squeezing on the upstroke and twisting over the head. His hips fuck into my fist, seeking pleasure.

Benji groans into my mouth, his teeth sinking into my lower lip as he erupts. I stroke him through it until he gently guides my hand away.

And then he pulls me into his arms, wrapping them around me, one hand low on my bump as he spoons me.

This part is nice, too. I like being in his arms. I like being wrapped up by him, surrounded by him. He makes me feel safe.

"I want this," he whispers.

Turning to look over my shoulder at him, I take in his serious expression. "Want what?"

"You. Us."

His throat works.

"I want there to be an us."

My hand covers his. "I want that, too."

seventeen

. . .

Benji

I'M WHISTLING when I walk through the door. Work was good today. Chet and Riv couldn't stop snickering at my good mood. I wasn't even upset when they convinced me that Estee should come to trivia tomorrow night. Because I want her there. I want her around all the time.

And I'm going to tell her. Tonight.

Except when I open the apartment door, the first thing I see is her prone body on the floor.

Fuck.

Terror runs through me as I race to her side. She's breathing, though it's not nearly as even as it should be. Her pulse is weak and thready.

What the fuck happened? I can't lose her.

I try to shake her shoulder. A soft whine comes from her throat and I exhale slowly. She's alive. She's breathing.

Okay. I can do this.

"Estee." I shake her more firmly.

She stirs. Her eyes blink open and she stares up at me with a frown.

"What's going on?" she asks. Her voice sounds slurred, like she has to work to get the words out.

"I could ask you the same thing." I let out a shaky laugh. "You're on the floor."

She blinks. "The floor?"

"Do you feel like you can sit up?"

Estee nods slowly. "Just—don't rush."

Gently, I help her shift to a sitting position, finding an applesauce pouch beside her.

"Does this happen often? The passing out?" My heart is still pounding.

She makes a soft noise. "It hasn't been this bad in a while."

"Is it because of last night?"

"The sex?" She giggles, some of her color returning. "No. I have blood pressure issues. I was getting myself something to eat when—"

Crushing her to me, I wrap my arms around her. My hands are starting to shake from the adrenaline.

"I'm fine, Benj," Estee says. "I'm okay."

"Are you, though? Or are you just saying what I want to hear?"

She opens her mouth, and I continue:

"Don't say you're fine again. You're always fine."

She pauses. "I think I'm really going to be okay."

I purse my lips. "I'd really feel better if we got a second opinion."

Her eyebrows go up. "A second opinion? Whose, yours?"

"No. A doctor." It's my turn to pause. "Can we, please? I'm worried about you."

Estee deflates. "Yeah. We can go get checked out."

"Why don't you have some applesauce first? Do you want crackers?"

She smiles indulgently. "Do we have the cheese crackers?"

Grabbing them from the cabinet, I open the little bag for her. She fishes out the cheese powder sandwich crackers. They remind me of childhood and sadness, but she loves them.

For her, I'd run out at midnight and buy out the whole store.

She has her snack and drinks some water, and then when she's feeling stable on her feet, I help her into a coat and down the stairs. I've already hailed a rideshare, so all that's left is to buckle her in and hold on tight.

Estee sets her hand on my knee. "I'm okay," she says again softly. "I'm really okay."

I take her hand in mine and she squeezes. Her grip is firm, and that little reminder of her strength helps to calm me.

"It's not just you I'm worried about," I admit. "You're fine, and I won't press you on that. But we should make sure the baby's okay, too."

Silently, she squeezes my hand again.

When we get to the ER, I stand beside her as she checks in, my hand on the small of her back. The waiting room is packed, but I'm not surprised when "Cohen, Esther" is called right away.

"Come with me," Estee says as they come to wheel her away.

I take her hand. "I'm not going anywhere."

The exam room is cold and bleak.

"Okay, so why don't you tell me what brought you in tonight?" the nurse asks. His name tag reads *Giovanni* and he looks young. Excessively young. But his name is followed by R.N., so I have to trust that he knows what he's doing.

Estee blows out a breath. "I'm thirty weeks and I'm having some issues with my blood pressure."

When she doesn't continue, I squeeze her hand. "I found her on the floor."

Giovanni doesn't blink. I admire him for that. "Well, hun, let's get you and the baby checked out. Who's your OB?"

"Dr. Singh."

He nods, making a note in her chart. "We'll call her, let her know what's going on."

Giovanni hooks up an IV and takes her vitals, then draws some blood. "We'll get a doctor in to see you soon," he promises before he leaves.

"This is a waste of time. I'm *fine*," Estee says again.

"Humor me, please." I look her in the eye. "I need to know you're okay." My hand moves to her belly. "This little one, too."

Her eyes soften. "C'mere," she says, tugging on my hand.

I'm not sure what she wants from me.

And then she's yanking on my shirt, pulling me forward until she can kiss me.

Do we get to do this now? Is this where we are now? *Sign me the fuck up.*

She half pulls me onto the bed and I find a way to awkwardly perch on the side. Estee shifts until I can join her, and when I wrap my arms around her, she sets her head on my chest.

"I'm trying really hard to convince myself that everything is fine," she says quietly. "Because if it's not fine, that means something is wrong, and I'm not sure I can handle something being wrong."

"I've got you. Let me worry for the both of us," I tell her.

She laughs. "I think you would regardless."

"That might be true." I kiss her temple. "You're not allowed to scare me like that again."

Exhaling slowly, she buries her face in my chest. "I'll try."

"We should probably talk," I say, trying to keep my tone as light and casual as possible.

Her entire body goes tense. "If you think so," she says coolly.

She tries to wiggle away, and I tighten my hold on her.

"I liked last night."

Estee swallows loudly. She looks up at me and then away again. "You did?"

"Yeah. It—we—I liked it," I say simply. "How are you feeling about it?"

"I mean, it was sex." She shrugs. "What am I supposed to say?"

Summoning all the strength I have, I venture, "Do you want it to happen again?"

"Yes," she says without hesitation. "Definitely."

All of the tension exits my body. "Good. Me, too."

Squinting up at me, she studies me carefully. "Did we just decide we're going to have sex again?"

"Well, not in a hospital bed," I joke, and she cracks a smile. "I'd like to decide some other things, too."

"Oh? Like what?"

"Like… can I take you out on a date?"

Her mouth drops open, and then she shakes her head. "You don't want to date me."

"I do, though."

"No. You just want to fuck around."

"That's the exact opposite of what I'd like, actually," I say evenly. "I'd like to build something with you. I want to give us a real chance."

Her eyes go wide. "I'm having a baby, Benji. I don't have time for—"

My hand moves to her belly. "I'm going to love your baby, Estee."

"But you don't know that. They'll be loud and cry all the time and—"

"And I'll still love them," I reiterate. "Because they're a part of you, and I love you."

Her jaw drops open. "Please tell me you didn't just say—"

"I love you." I tilt her chin until she meets my eyes. "I know it's fast, but that's why I don't want to fool around. I want more. And until I knew where you stood, we couldn't do anything. I had to protect my heart just like you need to protect yours."

"But last night…"

"I just want to make you happy. I don't want to fool around just for fun. I want to love you and hold you after, not have you run away."

She swallows. "I won't run away," she whispers.

"Good." Leaning down, I brush a soft kiss against her lips.

She sighs, melting into the kiss. I show her all the ways I love her, all the things I can't verbalize yet.

There's a knock on the exam room door, and we break apart to see the doctor in her white coat approaching. I scramble off the bed, reaching for Estee's hand.

"Good to see you again, Estee," Dr. Singh says. "Is this your partner?"

"Yes, hi. Benjamin Applebaum." I shake her hand. "You're taking good care of my girl. I appreciate it."

Dr. Singh gives me a smile. "Let's see what's going on."

She does a quick exam, asking questions along the way about Estee's eating habits, how much she's been drinking, and if she's been having other symptoms.

"I almost passed out yesterday," she admits.

"What?" I turn to her. "You didn't say anything!"

"I was with Arielle. I sat down for a bit and ate some pretzels. I was *fine*," she says.

Dr. Singh clucks. "I'd like to increase your monitoring. We'll meet weekly instead of biweekly going forward," she decides. "And you'll need more electrolytes."

Estee sighs. "Okay."

"If it doesn't improve, we'll talk about bed rest," she continues. "I don't think we're there yet. But if you don't take care of yourself…"

"She will," I tell her. "I'll make sure of it."

Dr. Singh laughs. "Good. We're all a team here. And all we want is a healthy Estee and a healthy baby."

She gives a few more instructions and makes some notes.

"Take care of yourself, Estee. And nice to meet you, Dad," she says as she leaves.

My heart stutters.

Dad.

And in that moment, I realize that's what I want. If I'm building something with Estee, it will naturally include the baby. They won't have a father involved in their lives.

But I could be that person. I would take care of them and be the best damn dad there is.

I turn to look at Estee, who's reaching for her pants.

"Don't read into it," she says.

"Read into what?" My voice comes out high-pitched. "Can we… can you sit down for a second?"

She looks at me, and whatever she sees on my face makes her pause and sit down with her pants around her thighs.

With a laugh, I help her finish dressing and take her hands.

"I want to be the baby's father," I tell her.

She blinks a few times. "What?"

"Look, I know it's fast. I know there's a lot to unpack," I tell her. "I love you, and I already love the baby. If you'd let me, I'd like to help you raise them. I don't just want to be your boyfriend. I want to be your *partner*. And that means I'd help raise the baby as if they were my own. Because as far as I'm concerned, they already are."

Estee swallows. "Are you sure?"

"I've never been more sure of anything in my life."

"Because it's—I'm—we're—"

"I love you." Squeezing her hand, I cup her face with my other hand. "I want to build a life with you, and that includes the baby. Your ex is out of the picture. The baby deserves a father. And if you'll let me, I'd like to be their father."

"You're serious."

I nod. "I don't have a ring, I don't know where we're

going beyond this. We already live together. I'd like for us to *be* together. A little family, raising our baby."

Tears well in her eyes. "I'd like that, too," she says, before she yanks me to her in a desperate kiss. My relief is overwhelming. She's okay, the baby is fine, and soon, the baby will be part mine. *Ours.*

A throat clears. "Okay, kids, I'm glad you're okay," Giovanni the nurse interrupts. "But you can't do that here."

"Let's go home," I say, and Estee lights up.

"Home," she agrees, taking my hand. I kiss her knuckles and help her into her coat, then take her hand again.

Home is wherever she is.

eighteen

· · ·

Estee

BENJI HANDS me a glass of sparking apple juice and kisses my cheek. "How are you doing?"

I consider for a moment, rather than answering *fine* outright. "I think I'm hungry," I decide.

"I'll make you a plate," he offers.

It's New Year's Eve and we're at Asher and Arielle's place for a low-key party. There are four or five other couples, there are games of Scrabble and Bananagrams going, and it's generally not terribly chaotic. Just what I need; a relaxing night with my friends.

Benji slides over to the table, ready to get me some more snacks, and Arielle comes up to take his place. She settles on the sofa beside me, tucking her feet underneath her.

"So things are going well, huh?" She smirks knowingly.

"Oh, shut up," I laugh, knocking her shoulder with mine.

After my hospital trip, they came over and the four of us spent the day together hanging out and watching college football. It was so freaking normal. I didn't realize how much I needed that.

Benji took me out to the movies last weekend. It was our first official date. It didn't feel like it, though. We've really gotten to know each other the last two months that we've been living together. We've both changed from who we were as kids at summer camp.

He still pulls my ponytail, though.

Last week, he sat me down and apologized for taunting me growing up. It's all water under the bridge as far as I'm concerned. He wasn't mean, he wasn't a bully—he was a snot-nosed kid who didn't know better, and now that he does, he certainly doesn't act that way.

Across the room, Benji has been pulled into conversation with Asher and Yoni, and I smile when I see him waving my little plate of food around. My nausea still isn't great, even with stronger meds, but he's gone out of his way to make sure I have safe foods around. And when I do get sick, he holds my hair out of my face and rubs my back.

Did I think my life would turn out this way? Living in Boston of all cities, not engaged, with a baby on the way, starting my life over at twenty-eight? Not at all.

Surrounded by my oldest friends, my boyfriend, our mutual friends… I wouldn't have it any other way. I finally feel at home here.

Asher—my friend since birth, my brother in everything but blood—crosses the room with Benji, and he gives me a wink and a smile as he scoops Arielle up and onto his lap.

My boyfriend—!—hands me the snack plate of crackers, olives, and tiny pickles. All I've wanted this week is salty and briny foods. Last night, he made pasta with a puttanesca olive and caper tomato sauce that was so good, it brought tears to my eyes.

Benji wants to be my baby's father. My mind is still blown.

He's been open that he doesn't want casual. I just hadn't realized how opposite of casual he wanted. And now… I'm not running away, I'm not afraid.

I love him.

He's gone out of his way to show me he loves me. It's the

little things, the way he brings me presents and cooks me comfort food and massages my back. It's the way he holds me and makes me feel safe. It's the way he's silently told me he loves me all this time. I just didn't see it.

My lower back twinges and I shift on the uncomfortable couch, trying to find a place that doesn't make fire spread through my lower body.

"You okay?" Benji murmurs, his forehead creased.

"Yeah. Just—*oh*." Another spasm. My hand falls to the side of my bump. "I don't think the baby is very happy right now."

His hand covers mine and he leans low. "Be nice to your mother," he says to my belly. The baby kicks under his touch, answering to his voice, and this time, a rebounding wallop of discomfort ricochets through me.

I shake my head. "Not helping."

He kisses my temple. "I'm sorry."

Asher looks worried. "Is it a contraction?"

"It's too soon," Arielle tells him. She turns to me. "It's too soon, right?"

Nodding, I take Benji's hand in mine. He squeezes gently.

"It must be Braxton Hicks," I say. "It hurts more in my back than anywhere else."

And of course the baby is two-stepping on my bladder. Again. A particularly violent kick makes the urge go from ever-present to right-fucking-now.

"I've got to pee," I announce. "Again."

With a smile, Benji helps me upright, and I kiss his cheek before making my way to the bathroom. Taking care of business, I finish up and wash my hands. I'm opening the door when I feel an intense wetness in my pants.

Did I miss? My bladder doesn't feel full.

Wetness seeps down my legs. My leggings are drenched now. The water—fluid?—keeps on coming. I can't control it. I try to cross my legs and that makes my stomach flutter—and *not* in a good way.

It starts to gush from between my legs, warm and sticky, and I do *not* like this feeling. My heart flutters at a pace that can't possibly be healthy. I feel dizzy and a little nauseous.

Oh, no. No, no, no.

This can't be what I think it is. It's too soon. I'm not due for another three weeks.

Dr. Singh said it *could* happen, that I'm technically ready any day now, but I thought there would be more time. I am so not ready for this.

Opening the bathroom door, I find Mara, who's waiting her turn.

"Get Benji," I tell her, and with wide eyes, she scuttles off to find him.

My boyfriend is at the door in moments, his face worried.

"What's wrong?" he asks immediately. "Are you okay?"

Taking a big breath, I try not to cry. "I think my water just broke."

His face goes slack for a moment before he clears his throat and claps twice.

"Okay, we've got this," he declares. "We can handle this."

"I can't." My voice sounds weak. I don't want to be help-less. But… "I can't do this."

"You can and you will," he says authoritatively, hands on my shoulders. "Are you okay if I take the lead on this?"

My laugh is weak as another strong cramp hits my back. "Sure. Whatever. Please do."

He springs into motion. Ushering me out of the bathroom, he directs me down the hall to Asher and Arielle's en suite, where he turns on the water.

"Wash off, and I'll get you new clothes," he says. He helps me take off my wet, dirty clothes before I step into the shower. When I get out, he's holding a pair of sweats and a t-shirt. The sweats are probably Arielle's, but the t-shirt is definitely Asher's. Even with my swollen belly, it's enormous on me, and it shouldn't feel weird to be wearing another man's t-shirt, but it does.

I want to wear Benji's t-shirts. Not Asher, my pseudo-brother. Only Benji's.

When we emerge, he ushers me directly down to the street, where a car is waiting for us. Benji buckles me in as another wave of discomfort rebounds through me. Unable to stop myself, I let out a whimper that turns into a groan of pain.

"Is she okay?" the driver asks.

"Just step on it," Benji mutters, rubbing my arm. "I gave Yoni my keys, he's going to grab your bag and meet us there."

Breathing through the pain, I nod. "It's in the front—"

"In the hallway closet," he finishes. "I told him to bring some applesauce pouches, too. You didn't get a chance to eat much at the party, and they probably won't let you eat once you get there."

My heart melts. He thought of everything.

"Thank you." I hope my tone conveys my sincere thanks, but my grimace at the next wave of nausea might not help. I squeeze his hand.

"I've got you, babe," Benji says. "I'm here for you."

The next half hour passes by in a blur. Getting to the hospital, being wheeled to a room in the maternity ward, changing into the itchy gown…

Benji is by my side through it all. When Yoni shows up an hour later, he goes to meet him and retrieve my bag, and is back within fifteen minutes. I'm not up for visitors.

I swallow. "If this is it…"

He squeezes my arm. "Do you want me to call your mom?"

We're not close—she has too many diagnoses to make that possible—but I still want her here.

"Yeah. But only if this is the real thing." I can't even say the word *labor*. "If it's a false alarm, I don't want to bother her."

"You're not a bother," Benji says. He drops a kiss to my forehead. "Do you want Mrs. Gold—Lydia—to come, too?"

Asher's mom is almost as much mine as she is his. She's infinitely more supportive. When I mentioned I split up with my ex, she asked how I was holding up, whereas my own mother just changed the subject.

"Are you okay with that?" I ask.

He shakes his head. "It's not my decision. My job is to support you. Your body, your baby. You get to decide who you surround yourself with."

The nurse comes in to check on me, and when she cheerfully announces that I'm four centimeters dilated, I nearly pass out.

"Call my mom," I tell Benji. "And Lydia."

He nods, pulling out his phone. I watch him through the open doorway as he paces while he talks to them. He's never met my mother. They've never spoken on the phone. She doesn't even know we're together. I can't imagine what kind of conversation they're having now.

And when he hangs up, he comes back into the room and pulls me into a hug.

"You are going to be a *terrific* mother," he announces.

I force a laugh. "My mom was that bad?"

"You are going to be awesome at it," he reiterates. "Mrs. Gold says she'll get on the first flight tomorrow."

Asher's mom has been an enormous help through all of this. It may be misguided, because she's upset she doesn't get to spend time with her own grandkids—she's estranged from her eldest son, Ash's brother—and because Asher doesn't have any kids yet, but I'll take all the support I can get.

But I want my mommy. Even if she doesn't really want to be there for me, I still want her here.

Another wave of pain. I breathe through it, but a tiny tear slips out.

I'm going to be the best damn mom to this baby. I'm going to love them and support them, even if I might disagree with their choices. Because the choice to make will be *theirs*. As long as they are safe and happy, I will love them and support them—no matter what.

Benji holds my hand and whispers words of affirmation to me. The clock hits midnight and he kisses me, soft and slow, then holds me in his arms.

The nurse comes to give me an epidural, but it doesn't dull the pain one bit. The hours pass in a blur of pain of discomfort. Benji is there through it all, even as the early morning hours turn into sunrise and then high noon. He doesn't leave my side.

And then it's time to push. A wave of pain. More nausea. I feel woozy.

When I hear a cry, I have to blink my eyes open. They feel so heavy. Impossibly heavy.

Then there's a loud beeping sound.

And then everything goes black.

nineteen

. . .

Benji

THE DOCTOR and nurses flurry into motion, pushing me out of the way as they get to Estee. My eyes fly to her, motionless on the bed, and then the little bundle they're putting into the clear plastic bassinet. They're getting ready to wheel it out when my brain jolts into action.

I'm in the way here.

I follow the nurse into the hallway. She turns when she hears my footsteps.

"Is the baby okay?" I ask. My voice is hollow.

The nurse beams. "A healthy baby boy. Six pounds, six ounces. Congratulations, Dad."

My heart stutters to a stop. *Dad.*

"Can I—I mean, can I see him?"

Taking a look around, the nurse moves closer to the nurse's station before parking the little carrier. She lifts the baby out and hands him to me.

And when I hold Estee's baby for the first time… Tears spring to my eyes.

The baby is swaddled in a little white blanket, his dark eyes cloudy and half-open. He's the most beautiful little thing I've ever seen.

"Hi, little one," I whisper. My voice comes out hoarse and rough. "They're taking good care of your mom. She's a fighter." He lets out a soft sigh. "And so are you."

The nurse squeezes my shoulder. "You'll be an excellent dad."

It still hasn't hit me that this is my kid now. My son.

When I told Estee I'd love her baby, I meant it. I didn't expect it to hit me over the head with a two by four, I figured it would take some time. Seeing him now, ten little fingers and ten little toes and ten times perfect… I can't fathom ever letting him go.

The baby shifts in my arms and I hold my breath, afraid to drop him. But he squirms and then gets comfortable, lips smacking.

I lose track of time. Everything zeroes in on this, on us.

This is my son. He might not be mine biologically, but he is emotionally. I would do anything for this baby. And I'll spend every damn day of the rest of my life making sure he knows that.

Footsteps make their way toward us, and I turn to see another nurse approaching. I recognize him as one of the nurses taking care of Estee.

"She's stable," he says. His eyes dart between me and the baby. "Do you want to see her?"

I swallow. "Can I bring him with me?" I don't want to be separated from him for a moment. "Does he have to go to the nursery?"

The nurse smiles. "He gets to meet his mom."

Gently placing the baby in the plastic carrier, I let the first nurse wheel him back.

Estee is sitting up in the bed, her face pale. She's sipping water and her eyes go wide when we approach.

"Is that…?"

At the nurses' prompting, I lift the baby and bring him to her.

"Estee, meet your son."

She immediately bursts into tears. She's smiling, though, and she makes grabby hands, so I place him in her arms.

Rounding the bed, I perch on the other side, and she leans into me, her head on my shoulder.

"Look at him," she whispers, her finger tracing the tip of his nose.

"He's perfect," I agree. "You did so good."

"I love you," she says quietly.

"I love him, too."

"No." Estee turns to look at me. "I love *you*."

I swallow thickly. "You're just saying that. It's the baby hormones. I won't hold you to it."

She shakes her head. "Benji, I *love* you. And it's not because of the baby. It's because of you."

Threading my hands through her sweaty ponytail, I hold her close and kiss her temple.

"I love you, and I love our son, and I love our perfect family," she says.

And when she kisses me… I think I'm finally starting to believe her.

A little squawk interrupts us, and we separate to see the baby starting to fuss. He squirms in his swaddle, desperately trying to be free.

A nurse approaches, and she shows Estee how to feed the baby, promising a lactation consultant will stop by soon. We sit for a bit, our little family.

I feel content. Complete, in a way I hadn't expected. I didn't think I was missing anything before. Now, I know what it means to have my heart so full it might burst.

My phone chimes, and for the first time in hours, I check it.

"Are you up for visitors?" I ask.

Estee pauses, deciding, as the baby makes gurgling, suckling sounds. "I think so."

I kiss her forehead. "I'll go grab them."

Asher and Arielle are in the lobby with his mother and Estee's mom. I haven't seen her since high school, but I'd recognize her anywhere. She and her daughter could be twins.

"How is she?" Asher asks worriedly.

"Doing okay," I answer, not sure if she wants people to know about her blood pressure bottoming out. Giving birth isn't a spectator sport; it's a medical procedure. "He's beautiful."

Arielles squeaks, covering her mouth with her hands. "It's a boy?"

Asher reaches out and grips my arm. "Congratulations, Benj. I'm so happy—for both of you."

Mrs. Cohen purses her lips. "Can we see her?"

Nodding, I swallow my nerves. "She's just through here."

Mrs. Gold—Lydia—tugs me into a hug. "It's good to see you again, Benji," she says. "I'm so glad you were here for our Estee."

I spent more than a few school breaks at Asher's house growing up. My home life wasn't great and the Golds seemed to know that. I'm not sure how much Asher told them. We spent all summer together at camp and he insisted on me visiting for every school break.

Estee being there was a big reason I went. But Asher was there for me throughout it all, too. He was such a positive influence on me when I needed it most.

I wouldn't be where I am today without Asher Gold.

He's Estee's brother in everything except blood. They've been best friends since they were born. Growing up, they did everything together, even in the "girls are icky" stage. When hormones got involved, he made sure that anyone who wanted to date her had to meet his approval.

It means a lot that he gave it to me. To us.

Estee is sitting up in the bed. The baby—still no name—has finished feeding and he's in her arms, she's gazing down at him again.

I knock on the doorframe and she jolts, her smile deepening at the sight of her assembled family.

Mrs. Cohen rushes forward. "Let me see him," she says. "He's a boy?"

Estee nods, swallowing. "There's some hand sanitizer over there." She points.

"Don't point, it's rude," her mother snaps, making no move. She's standing absurdly close, almost breathing on the baby.

Estee flinches.

Asher steps forward. "We'll all sanitize," he says. "I'm so proud of you, Es." He moves toward the sanitizer dispenser, covering his hands liberally. "Let me see my nephew."

Asher perches on the end of her bed and Estee swallows as she lowers the baby into his arms.

"I was—we were thinking," she says, reaching for me, and I take her hand in mine. "We wanted you to be the baby's godparents. If anything happens to us…"

In Jewish tradition, we don't have officially named godparents. It's not a thing in our culture.

I squeeze her hand. Something almost *did* happen to her just a few hours ago.

"Absolutely," Arielle says.

Asher's eyebrows go up. "Really? You'd want that?" He passes the baby to her.

She nods. "I'd rather nothing happen to either of them. In the worst case scenario… I'd do anything for this baby. In fact, I'm feeling quite murdery."

Alarmed, Estee demands, "Give me back the baby."

But Arielle shakes her head. "I won't hurt him. I would commit murder for this baby. I'll do anything to protect him."

Estee grins, sinking back into her pillows. "I'll allow it."

"Do you have a name yet?" Lydia asks, tears in her eyes.

"I was thinking Levi, after my dad," Estee says. He passed away a few years ago. In the Ashkenazi Jewish tradition, we name after the dead. It's our way of honoring them.

"What about a middle name?" Mrs. Cohen pushes. She practically snatches the baby out of Arielle's arms.

"Samuel," Estee says.

"Where'd you get that?" Asher asks, cocking his head.

"It was Benji's grandfather's name," she says.

When we traded childhood stories a few weeks ago, she asked about the grandparents who left me their apartment. My Grandpa Sam was my hero, my best friend. And now she's naming her son, *our* son, after him... A tear comes to my eye, and I wipe it away.

"He's beautiful, Estee," Lydia says, standing over her long-time friend's shoulder. "Levi Samuel. Beautiful."

Levi starts to fuss, and I lift him from my future mother-in-law's arms, returning him to Estee's. He nuzzles into her and sighs.

I sit on the side of the bed and Estee leans against me. Squeezing her shoulder, I glance down at the sleepy face of our son. My finger trails over his downy cheek, and my heart gives a thump.

"I love you," I whisper, not sure which of them I'm saying it to. Maybe both.

Estee turns her head, giving me a soft kiss. "I love you, too."

There's a lot up in the air. I don't know the first thing about being a father. I'm not ready for marriage—Estee and I have only been together for a month. I don't know what I'm doing.

But when I look down at Levi, *our* son... I know it's all going to be okay. We'll figure it out together. Whether we get married, whether we stay a couple… I know we'll get through it. Because we'll be together.

Levi lets out a little yawn, Estee makes a soft noise, and my heart flutters with warmth.

Yeah. We're going to be alright.

epilogue

. . .

Estee

THERE'S A SHRIEK, and then laughter, and as my heart rate starts to regulate, I hear a loud *thud* and then a wail.

"I've got it," Benji calls from the other room.

Sitting in the nursery, I continue feeding our son. He's got this handled.

When he enters the room a few minutes later, it's with Levi on his back and our three-year-old daughter hanging by her feet.

"I think this one belongs to you," he says, tossing Hannah gently onto the beanbag chair she's claimed as her own. She giggles uproariously.

"Daddy, daddy, my turn," five-year-old Levi demands.

With a chuckle, Benji swings him off his back and tosses him onto the beanbag, too. His smile stretches from ear to ear.

"How's the peanut?" he asks, his finger trailing over little Bryan's downy cheek.

"Feeling better. His fever's gone down."

The baby's been teething, which makes it super fun for everyone in the house. Levi could sleep through a tornado siren, but Hannah is a light sleeper, so every time Bryan wakes up, so does she. Even though her room is across the house from his. Benji will tend to her while I feed and change Bryan, so we're both perpetually exhausted.

After Levi was born, we soon outgrew Benji's two bedroom apartment. It was great, we had some wonderful memories there, but we needed more space. We found a little house in the suburbs a few streets over from where Arielle and Asher bought their house. Our kids play together nearly every day.

I still work from home, now for a different law firm. Still reviewing contracts, still bored silly. But it's the good kind of bored, because it means I have mental energy at the end of the day.

We tied the knot shortly before Levi's first birthday, celebrating both at the same time. The wedding was never something that I dreamed about; it was the marriage that would come after, the commitment.

And every day since, Benji has proven that he's committed to me, to our family. At his insistence, it's his name on Levi's birth certificate. When he's older, we'll tell him about my ex, and he can pursue a relationship with him if he so desires. I won't prevent him from seeking him out. In the meantime, I'm going to show him exactly what a loving, positive relationship between his parents looks like.

I haven't heard from my ex. Not that I'm surprised. He didn't even reach out at my due date. It's like he's washed his hands of the situation. I check his Instagram every once in a while. He has a new woman on his arm every few months, and they keep getting progressively younger as he gets older. I guess I dodged a bullet there.

When Bryan's done feeding, I burp him and change him, and his gummy baby smile beams up at me.

There's a hand on the back of my neck, and I lean into Benji, taking his silent support.

"You did good with this one, babe," he says, tickling the baby's tummy.

Bryan giggles and then spits up. I sigh.

"I've got it," he says, tightening his hand around the back of my neck. "You go take your bubble bath."

"But—"

"I can handle the three of them on my own," he says in a calm, soothing voice. "Go. I got you new bath salts."

He likes to buy me presents. We had to have a sit-down conversation about it. At one point, I had seven different bath soaps and salts sets, all of them unopened. I've been better at taking time for myself, but there's only so many baths I can take!

Now, he buys me experiences. A day at the museum. Tickets to a hockey game. A season subscription to the theater. He'll still come home with a trinket or two, every now and then, though now he makes sure to get things the kids will enjoy, too. There's nothing like a special cookie from the bakery or a new ball to get them excited.

He still gets me excited. He still gets *me*. Benji knows me in a way nobody else ever has. He's there for me every single day, through thick and thin, and he's made clear he'll be by my side for the rest of our lives. There's nobody else I want to share this life with.

And now…

He drops a kiss to my temple and then picks up the baby, cuddling him for a moment. My heart melts.

"I've got this," Benji repeats. "Go take your bath. Relax. I'll be here when you're done."

At the doorway, I stop and look back at them. When I got pregnant with Levi, when I moved to Boston, I never thought my life would turn out this way. I never expected my summer camp rival Benji Applebaum to be the person to turn my world upside down. I never planned on our life together.

I'm so glad it happened this way. I wouldn't change it for the world.

what's next?

Thank you for reading Twinkle. This story is near and dear to my heart. I appreciate your taking the time to read it!

Want the famous brisket recipe? You can get it here, with my family's adaptions.

about the author

Allie is a queer and AuDHD writer with a hyper-fixation on inclusivity and representation. She loves the color purple, Michigan football, and the Boston Bruins. When she's not absorbed by a book, she likes to spend time with her nephews.

Born and raised in Southern California, she now calls South Carolina home. She is allergic to the cold, rain, snow, and mosquitos.

also by allie lasky

Meet the Neurospicy Book Club in THE THOUGHT OF YOU: Falling for my Grumpy Roommate, where Johanna finds out she's autistic… because her happy-go-lucky new roomie (and reformed playboy ex-football player) has to tell her.

———

The story continues with PUCK ME TWICE, a second chance, fake dating romance featuring autistic hockey player Sven and the woman he hasn't been able to forget since their one night stand… when he gave her his virginity.

———

Want to see how it all started? Read <u>THE GAME PLAN</u> to meet sweet cinnamon roll football player Miles and the feisty sorority girl who stole his heart.

www.ingramcontent.com/pod-product-compliance
Lightning Source LLC
Chambersburg PA
CBHW061354310726
48974CB00001B/333